"You need to feel close to someone right now, and I'm here."

"It's all right, Esteban. I understand." Anna unbuttoned his shirt and slid it from his shoulders, then moved back into his arms and pressed her body against his.

Esteban rubbed his cheek against her silky hair. The arms holding Anna this time had a gentle strength. "I'm glad you're with me," he said quietly.

Anna leaned back and looked into his eyes.

Esteban trailed his fingers over the smooth skin of her cheek, his eyes following their movement. "How is it that I, who never needed anyone before, now find that I need you very much?" His eyes moved to hers. "And what am I going to do about that need when you're gone?"

"It's not me," she said softly. "It's the circumstances. It's tonight, not tomorrow."

Esteban put his finger under her chin and gazed at her lovely face. Ever so slowly, he lowered his mouth to hers.

Dear Reader,

When I think of the month of June, I summon up images of warm spring days with the promise of summer, joyous weddings and, of course, the romance that gets the man of your dreams to the point where he can celebrate Father's Day.

And that's what June 1990 is all about here at Silhouette Romance. Our DIAMOND JUBILEE is in full swing, and this month features *Cimarron Knight*, by Pepper Adams—the first book in Pepper's *Cimarron Stories* trilogy. Hero Brody Sawyer gets the shock of his life when he meets up with delightful Noelle Chandler. Then in July, don't miss *Borrowed Baby*, by Marie Ferrarella. Brooding loner Griffin Foster is in for a surprise when he finds that his sister has left him with a little bundle of joy!

The DIAMOND JUBILEE—Silhouette Romance's tenth anniversary celebration—is our way of saying thanks to you, our readers. To symbolize the timelessness of love, as well as the modern gift of the tenth anniversary, we're presenting readers with a DIAMOND JUBILEE Silhouette Romance title each month, penned by one of your favorite Silhouette Romance authors. In the coming months, many of your favorite writers, including Lucy Gordon, Dixie Browning, Phyllis Halldorson and Annette Broadrick, are writing DIAMOND JUBILEE titles especially for you.

And that's not all! There are six books a month from Silhouette Romance—stories by wonderful authors who time and time again bring home the magic of love. During our jubilee year, each book is special and written with romance in mind. June brings you *Fearless Father*, by Terry Essig, as well as *A Season for Homecoming*, the first book in Laurie Paige's duo, *Homeward Bound*. And much-loved Diana Palmer has some special treats in store in the months ahead.

I hope you'll enjoy this book and all the stories to come. Come home to romance—Silhouette Romance—for always!

Sincerely,

Tara Hughes Gavin
Senior Editor

BRITTANY YOUNG

The Seduction
of Anna

Silhouette *Romance*

Published by Silhouette Books New York

America's Publisher of Contemporary Romance

SILHOUETTE BOOKS
300 E. 42nd St., New York, N.Y. 10017

ISBN: 0-373-08729-2

First Silhouette Books printing June 1990

Printed in the U.S.A.

Silhouette Romance

BRITTANY YOUNG

lives and writes in Racine, Wisconsin. She has traveled to most of the countries that serve as the settings for her romances and finds the research into the language, customs, history and literature of these countries among the most demanding and rewarding aspects of her writing.

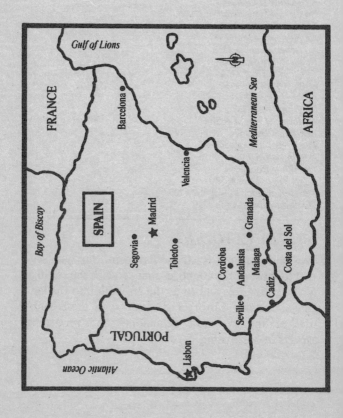

Chapter One

Anna Bennett sped down the long, curving driveway of her aunt and uncle's Long Island, New York country estate, past dozens of cars parked along its length, bringing her rented sports car to a screeching stop in front of the tall white pillars that lined the veranda. Climbing out of the car, she reached in through the open top of the vehicle to grab her suitcase, briefcase and portable computer. She then ran up the stairs and through the open front door.

The butler smiled affectionately when he saw her, and took her suitcase and computer. "Miss Anna, we were afraid you weren't going to get here on time."

Anna unself-consciously hugged the kindly butler she'd known for most of her life. "Hello, Peter. If my plane had made just one more circle over the airport, I wouldn't have, believe me. Where's Hayley?"

"Your cousin is in her room getting into her wedding gown. She's been asking about you every ten minutes."

"Oh, dear. I'd better let her know I'm here. Did my father arrive yet?"

"Mr. Bennett arrived yesterday evening."

"Good. Thank you, Peter." Anna dashed up the stairs and knocked on her cousin's door.

"Mother?" Hayley called.

"No, it's just me," Anna said as she opened the door and peeked around the edge.

Hayley, looking ravishing in lace and satin, turned away from the mirror and squealed as soon as she saw Anna. "Thank God you're here!" She rushed into Anna's open arms. "Where have you been? I was frantic!"

"To make a long story short, my flight from Rome got canceled. I couldn't get another flight out for twenty-four hours, and then that one was late." She paused, deliberately stopping the flow of words. "I'm so sorry I missed the dinner last night. I would have been here, if it had been at all possible."

"Don't you think I know that? Besides, it wasn't really all that important. I'm just so glad you're here now. My wedding wouldn't have been the same without you." Hayley stepped back and smiled at Anna. They might have been just cousins, but sisters were never closer than the two of them. Since childhood, each had known what the other was thinking before any words were spoken. No matter how far away Anna was—and she was almost always traveling around the world with her father—she'd been able to sense when Hayley needed her. The telephone would ring or a letter would arrive. It was the same with Hayley. It was a bond that had grown stronger over the years.

Hayley suddenly focused on what Anna was wearing, and her smile transformed into a look of panic. "You're not dressed for the wedding!"

Anna looked down at herself and then back at her cousin. "I just this minute got here."

Hayley put her hand to her breast, closed her eyes and took a deep breath. "What does a heart attack feel like?"

A smile lit Anna's lovely eyes. "Oh Hayley, relax. Everything's going to be fine. People get married every day."

"That's easy for you to say. All you have to do is walk down the aisle ahead of me, show up at the reception, and then get back to your life. This *is* my life."

"And you're going to love it. I know I've only met him once, but Marcos seems like a wonderful man."

Hayley exhaled a long breath and her expression softened. "Yes, he is. I'm very lucky."

"So's he."

"Oh Anna," Hayley said as she hugged her again. "I really am glad you're here. I don't know what I would have done if you hadn't made it."

"You would have gotten married as planned—and never spoken to me again."

"This is true."

"Is there anything I can do for you before I get dressed?"

"Everything's under control."

"Right," Anna said with a dry smile.

Hayley turned to look at herself in the mirror. "Just look at me," she moaned. "My hair is a wreck."

"Your hair is perfect." Anna's was the voice of reason. "Where's your veil?"

Hayley pointed to the bed.

Anna picked up the confection of chiffon and lace and centered it on top of her cousin's head, smoothing out the folds, then stood back to look. Her green eyes quickly filled with tears as she looked at her. "Hayley, you're the most beautiful bride I've ever seen." She placed her hands on Hayley's shoulders and turned her toward the mirror again. "Look at yourself."

The images of the two women reflected couldn't have been more different. Anna's golden hair hung in a silken wave to her shoulders while Hayley's short, dark hair was cropped into thick curls. Hayley's brown eyes were somber, while Anna's lovely green ones sparkled. "I hope Marcos thinks so."

"You and I both know that you could be wearing sackcloth and ashes and Marcos would still think you were the most beautiful woman at the wedding."

Hayley smiled. It was impossible not to. "You're right, and I'm being silly."

"You're being human."

"Now there's an indictment if I ever heard one."

"You know what I mean."

"I know." She turned from the mirror. "Well now that you've calmed me down, you'd better get dressed.

Mother's going to be up here in a few minutes, and I wouldn't want to be you if you're not ready."

"Is Aunt Catherine nervous, too?"

"Let me put it this way: next to Mom, I'm the Rock of Gibraltar."

Anna laughed as she tried to picture her dignified and usually calm aunt reduced to a bundle of nerves. "I hear you. Where's my dress?"

"Draped over the bed in your room."

"All right." Anna headed for the door. "I don't suppose I have time for a shower?" she asked hopefully.

Hayley raised an expressive brow. "You can't be serious."

"Sorry. Just thought I'd ask. I'll hurry."

As soon as Anna had closed the door behind her, she quickly covered the distance down the hall to the room she used whenever she visited. The black satin dress was on the bed, just as Hayley had said. Anna quickly stripped out of the clothes she was wearing and stepped into the carpeted bathroom. After soaking a washcloth in cool water, she wrung it out and held it to her face. If only she could learn the fine art of sleeping on planes, the constant travel she'd been doing wouldn't tire her so much. As it was, she'd been up for forty-eight hours straight, flying, negotiating, writing reports and flying some more, and it was catching up with her. If she could just manage to keep on moving, she might make it through the rest of the day. She turned the cloth over to a cool side and pressed it against her eyes again, then hung it up and went back into the bedroom to get ready.

The black satin dress was beautiful. The snug-fitting bustier top left her pale shoulders bare. The waist was dropped, with a white ribbon of satin and delicate white rose that rode low on her hip. The skirt flared out to just above her knees. She managed to pull the zipper halfway up the back of the dress, but then it stuck. Anna tugged and tugged at it, finally moving to the mirror and looking over her shoulder while she worked on unsticking the zipper. Nothing worked. She needed help. Swearing softly under her breath about the wasted time, she whipped open the door—and crashed headlong into a solid wall of chest. The chest had arms that reached out and caught her by the shoulders to keep her from falling backward. "I'm so sorry!" Anna gasped, as she regained her balance and looked up into rich honey-colored eyes set into a carved face. Her heart involuntarily missed a beat.

"Are you all right?" the man asked in a deliciously accented voice.

"Yes. Thank you for catching me."

The groove in his cheek deepened. "It wasn't a problem, believe me. Are you by any chance Anna Bennett?"

"I am."

His hands fell to his sides. "How do you do? I'm Esteban Alvarado, Marcos's brother. Hayley's mother asked me to escort you downstairs."

She smiled, a little embarrassed, unintentionally charming the man. "I'm sorry. My aunt is forever trying to make sure I'm well taken care of. In point of fact, I'm perfectly capable of taking care of myself. If there's someplace or someone with whom you'd rather be, please don't feel any kind of obligation toward me."

"I'm quite content in your company, Anna Bennett. Are you ready?"

"Ready?" Anna suddenly remembered why she'd come into the hall in the first place. "Oh, dear."

The Spaniard looked at her curiously.

"My zipper is stuck."

"Perhaps I can help. Turn around."

No one was more surprised by her hesitation than Anna.

The groove in his cheek deepened even more. "I'm very good with zippers."

Anna's smile flashed unexpectedly.

"Shame on you for what you're thinking, young lady."

"I didn't say a word."

"You didn't have to." He put his hand on her shoulders and turned her around.

There was a slight tug, then she felt the tightening of the dress as the zipper slid smoothly up her back. Anna glanced up at him over her shoulder. "Thank you."

The Spaniard inclined his dark head.

Trying not to appear as self-conscious as she felt, Anna went back into her room. "I'll just be a minute," she said as she pulled her jewelry case out of her luggage and removed a delicate diamond necklace and matching earrings. Moving to her mirror, Anna clipped on the earrings and fastened the necklace. Then she quickly brushed her hair, added a little color to her lips and cheeks, and slipped into her high heels.

"All right," she said as she left her room and closed the door behind her. "Now I'm ready."

Esteban's look seemed to take all of her in at once. As he reached out to adjust her necklace, his fingertips brushed against the vulnerable spot at the base of her throat, sending a shiver of awareness through her. Anna stepped back abruptly, raising her hand protectively to her throat. Surprised, her eyes locked with the Spaniard's.

A muscle in Esteban's cheek tightened as he looked at her. Without saying anything, he took her hand and held it for a moment before drawing it through the crook of his arm. His eyes moved over her face, then he turned his head and looked straight ahead as the two of them started walking.

Anna exhaled, suddenly realizing that she'd been holding her breath. She trembled noticeably. Esteban pulled her arm more tightly through his without breaking his stride.

Forcing her attention away from the Spaniard, she tried to pay attention to her surroundings. She'd been in too much of a hurry to notice anything when she'd arrived, but now, as she and Esteban descended the stairs, she saw just how breathtaking everything was. Bright red flowers and white ribbons were wound along the banisters. Long-stemmed red and white roses filled huge vases throughout the foyer.

They left the foyer and walked through the living room and out the doors leading to the lawn. White lawn chairs, filled with guests, lined either side of a center aisle. Tall white poles topped with more flowers and ribbons stood along the aisle, one next to every other row of chairs. There was a small orchestra off to one side, playing classical music. On the other side, about five hundred feet away, enormous forest-green-and-white striped tents sheltered white-clothed tables. "This is beautiful," Anna said quietly. "My aunt really outdid herself."

Esteban gazed around the lawn as well, but said nothing.

"Anna! You made it!"

She turned to find her father walking toward her, his arms outstretched. Anna hugged him. "Barely."

"Did you get held up in the meeting with Domenici?"

"No. At the airport."

"So the meeting went all right?"

"So-so. I think you're going to have to come up with more money before he'll sell his controlling stock to you. I wrote up a report on the plane. We can go over it later." She turned apologetically to Esteban. "I'm sorry. This isn't really the time to discuss business. Have you two met?"

Her father shook Esteban's hand. "Yes, as a matter of fact, we have," he said coolly. "How are you this morning, Doctor?"

"Fine, thank you."

Anna looked from one man to the other. Something was definitely going on between the two of them. It wasn't that they were unfriendly. It was more like they were sizing each other up. "Did I miss something here?" she asked.

Before either of the men could answer, Hayley's mother—and Anna's father's sister—hurried down the stairs to where they were standing. "Darling, I'm so glad you made it," she said as she hugged Anna. "It wouldn't have been the same without you." She stepped back, took a breath and lifted her hand to her still-brown hair. "How do I look?"

"A little frazzled but lovely, Aunt Catherine," Anna said with a smile.

"Frazzled being the operative word. Honestly Anna," she said sotto voce, "when this is all over, I'm going to sleep for a week." She turned to her brother and resumed her normal tone. "Charles, it's time for everyone to take his place. I'd appreciate it if you'd escort me down the aisle to my seat."

Charles took his sister's arm and gave it an affectionate squeeze. "Stop worrying. Everything's going to be fine."

Catherine leveled her gaze at her brother as they started to walk. "You're calm now, but wait until it's your daughter who's getting married."

"Not my Anna," he said with a wink at his daughter. "She's like me. Married to the business."

Esteban looked at his watch and then at Anna. "Please excuse me. I have to get Marcos. I'll see you after the wedding."

"Of course." Anna watched as his broad shoulders disappeared around the corner. What an utterly intriguing man.

A moment later the music changed. The bridesmaids came together as a group and talked in low whispers as they waited. When Hayley and her father appeared at the top of the stairs, Anna looked up at her nervous cousin and smiled encouragingly. Hayley tried to smile back but couldn't quite pull it off. She looked as though she were about to cry, and a moment later Anna felt tears burning in the back of her own eyes. She had to will herself not to let them fall.

The music changed yet again. The bridesmaids stopped talking and walked down the aisle. At a nod from Uncle John, Anna also started down the aisle.

Marcos and his brother were already there. Esteban's eyes were on Anna, with an intensity that overcame her will not to look at him. Once her eyes met his, she couldn't look away. At least she couldn't until she had to turn aside, but even then she could feel his gaze on her, burning its way through her.

It was strange. Anna was used to being looked at by men, but this was different. Or perhaps it was the way she was reacting to him that was different. She was so aware of him. There was an energy about him that she could actually feel.

But now wasn't the time to think about that. This was Hayley's moment, and just seconds later her cousin walked down the aisle on the arm of her father.

Anna watched Hayley, then turned her head to look at Marcos to see what his reaction was.

She wasn't disappointed. His dark eyes were riveted on his bride-to-be. She could see the love, and so could Hayley. The woman who minutes before had been so nervous that she could barely smile, gazed into her lover's eyes and was suddenly at peace. Anna could see it in the relaxation of Hayley's body. Marcos held his hands out to Hayley. She put both of hers into his. They gazed at one another for a moment, and then she stood beside him while her father took his seat next to her mother.

Anna's thoughts were so scattered as she stood there that it seemed as though the ceremony was over as soon as it began. She had no idea what had been said. Suddenly Hayley and Marcos were walking down the aisle. Esteban held out his arm and Anna slipped her hand through it as they followed the bride and groom. As soon as they were back in the house, Hayley held out her arms to Anna. "I did it," she whispered.

Anna hugged her tightly. "I wish you all the best and much happiness."

"What about me?" Marcos asked with a smile.

Anna hugged him, as well. "You're a wonderful man. I can't think of anyone I'd rather see Hayley married to."

Esteban kissed Hayley on either cheek and hugged his brother. "If you two want a few minutes alone before the reception, you'd better take them now."

Grinning at each other, Marcos and Hayley clasped hands, turned and ran toward the unoccupied study.

Anna's eyes followed them dreamily. "It must be wonderful to feel that way."

"Surely you must have, at some point in your life."

She shook her head. "Oh, I've had an infatuation or two, but that's not the same thing."

A corner of the Spaniard's mouth lifted.

Anna looked at him curiously. "Why are you smiling?"

"You amuse me."

"I think I'm offended."

His smile grew. "No you're not. Let's join the others."

Before they could get away, Anna's father spotted her. "Excuse us," he said to Esteban, "but my daughter and I have some things we need to discuss." Taking her by the arm, he all but pulled her away from the other man.

"Dad," she protested as he took her into the living room, "whatever it is, I'm sure it could wait."

"I want to know more about your talks with Domenici."

"I already capsulized them for you. If you want more detail, read my report. Everything is in it."

"Go get it and we'll go over it right now."

Anna looked at her father in disbelief. "We're at a wedding. The report will still read the same way tomorrow. What's really going on?"

Her father took a cigarette from a silver case and placed it between his lips. "I don't know what you mean."

"Yes you do. You just used Domenici as an excuse to get me away from Esteban Alvarado."

Charles Bennett lit his cigarette. "I concede the point."

"Why?"

"I don't like the man."

"Why not?"

"He's different from us."

"Meaning that he's a doctor and not a businessman?"

"Precisely."

"That's certainly an indictment."

"Oh, Anna, it's more than that. The man is trouble; I sense it."

Anna was surprised into silence. She'd never seen her father act like this before. Standing in front of him, she gently removed the cigarette from his mouth. "First of all, your doctor told you to stop smoking. And secondly, I choose my own friends—just as you choose yours." She kissed his cheek. "Now stop scowling."

"I'm not scowling," he said with a scowl.

Anna tried not to smile, but couldn't quite manage it. "I stand corrected."

"And Esteban Alvarado aside, I want that report tomorrow, young lady."

"You'll have it. Now if it's all right with you, I'd like to rejoin the party." She turned to leave.

"Anna?"

She looked over her shoulder at her father. "Ummhmm?"

"Remember what I said about the Spaniard."

Anna stood there for a quiet moment, then turned and left just in time to see Marcos and Hayley disappearing through the double doors leading to the lawn. She followed them, stopping here and there to speak with people she knew.

But as happy as the occasion was, Anna needed some time to herself. She'd been on the go for two days, only to arrive here to jump immediately into a wedding, and she just wanted to be alone for a few minutes.

Crossing the lawn, she made her way down a terraced hillside to a stretch of sandy beach that lined the ocean. The light breeze lifted her silky hair away from her neck. Anna sighed with contentment, as she raised her face to the fading sun and closed her eyes. She'd been dreaming about this beach for months.

Slipping out of her shoes, her stockinged toes sinking into sand that was growing cool on top but remained warm beneath the surface, she walked slowly down the beach, her shoes dangling casually from her fingers.

When she found her favorite flat-topped boulder, Anna climbed up and sat on the edge. It hung over the water, too high for her to dangle her feet in its cool blueness.

If she could just close her eyes for a few minutes, it would make all the difference.

Lying back on the rock, aware that she was going to have to dust herself off before going back to the reception, Anna folded her hands over her stomach and closed her eyes. The sun warmed her bare skin, making her even more drowsy. The sound of the waves washing against the rock... She couldn't remember ever feeling quite so comfortable. Within minutes, she was sound asleep. And she stayed asleep even after the sun had sunk into the horizon and the moon offered its glow over the softly rippling water.

"Anna," said a soft, deep voice, pronouncing her name as though it were spelled *Ahnna*. A hand gently touched her hair.

Anna turned her head so that her cheek was cradled in the hand, then slowly opened her eyes. Esteban Alvarado was beside her, gazing down at her.

She lay there, completely still, and looked at him. "What are you doing here?" she asked sleepily.

"I saw you leave the reception. You were gone for a long time and I got worried, so I came looking for you."

Anna sat up and rubbed her eyes. "Thank you. I probably would have slept all night. What time is it?"

"Almost midnight."

"Midnight! I had no idea it was so late. I hope Hayley hasn't noticed."

"She has."

"I'd better get back." She searched the surface of the rock with her hands.

Esteban held up her shoes. "Looking for these?"

Anna smiled. "Thank you again."

"Give me your foot."

She slid back on the rock and raised her foot. Esteban held her slender ankle in one hand and slipped the pump onto her foot, then did the same with the other pump. Anna liked the firmness of his touch. There was no hesitation. And she liked the warmth of his fingers against her skin.

Her eyes moved over the top of his head. "I bet you're a good doctor."

Esteban looked up at her. "What makes you think so?"

"Your hands. They're very gentle."

"As it happens, you're right. I'm good at what I do." He jumped from the rock, and held out his arms for Anna.

She slid part of the way down until his hands could reach her waist, then slipped easily into his arms. Instead of setting her down, he swung her up so that he had one of his arms under her knees and the other around her back. "What are you doing?" she asked as he began walking.

"While you were sleeping, the tide came in and soaked the sand. You'll be a mess beyond cleaning if you try to walk on it, with or without shoes."

Anna's arm was draped around Esteban's neck. Her face was close to his. She could smell the clean scent of him.

He turned his head and looked into her eyes. "And what are you thinking, Anna Bennett?"

"That I'm remarkably comfortable, considering I'm in the arms of a man I barely know."

"Are you flirting with me?"

Anna thought for a moment. "Yes, I believe I am."

"Do you flirt with many men?"

Anna thought again. "No," she finally said in all honesty, "the fact is that I almost never flirt."

"Good."

"Good?"

"Yes. I don't ordinarily like flirtatious women."

"Ordinarily?"

"You, I like."

Her eyes smiled into his. "This is an interesting conversation. I like you, too."

Esteban set her on her feet at the bottom of the hill. "Turn around."

Anna obediently turned.

"Black dresses and rock climbing were never intended to go together," he said as he brushed the sand from her dress.

"Am I a terrible mess?" she asked as she looked over her shoulder and down at herself in the dim light that came from above.

"Do you want an honest answer or a tactful one?"

"Uh-oh. If I have to choose, things must be pretty bad."

"You look as though someone shook a dust mop at you."

Anna strained to get a better look at the back of her dress.

"Stop wriggling."

"I'm not wriggling."

"Yes, you are." His hand brushed over the material of her dress several more times and then he rose. "There. That's as good as it's going to get."

"Perhaps I should go to my room and change."

"I don't think you have time before Hayley and Marcos leave for their honeymoon."

"Then I guess we'll just have to go and face everyone."

"We?"

Anna started up the hill. "You realize, of course, that the fact that we both disappeared from the reception and then returned together, with me in a state of disarray, is going to cause everyone to think you've had your way with me."

"I don't think so."

She stopped on her step, turned and looked down at him. "Why not?"

Esteban stood on the step below her so that they were eye level. "Because, Anna, if I'd had my way with you, you would be in considerably more disarray—and we would both look a lot happier."

Anna didn't smile as her eyes moved over his face, coming to rest at last on his carved mouth.

He cupped her chin in the palm of his hand and looked into her eyes. His lips were mere inches from hers. Anna could feel the accelerated beating of her heart as he rubbed his thumb lightly over her lips, his eyes still on hers.

"Are you going to kiss me?" she asked.

"Would you like me to?"

Their lips were almost touching. She could feel his warm breath. "I think I would."

He came achingly closer. Her skin tingled from his nearness.

Then he straightened away from her.

Anna looked at him curiously.

A corner of his mouth lifted. "I think," he said softly, "that if I were to start kissing you, I wouldn't want to stop." Releasing her chin, he put his hands on her shoulders and turned her around. "Go on. Let's mingle with the rest of the guests and be the sociable creatures we're supposed to be."

When they got to the top of the hill the guests were gathered around Marcos and Hayley. Both of them had already changed into traveling clothes. Hayley spotted Anna almost instantly and made her way through the people to her. "Where have you been?"

"Sleeping on my rock. I'm sorry, Hayley. I didn't mean to be gone so long. I'd probably still be there if it weren't for Esteban finding me."

Hayley hugged her. "Don't worry about it. You didn't really miss anything. Just some of the best food and the finest music in the world. And don't let the cost of all of this bother you, either."

"Thanks for putting my mind at ease," Anna said dryly.

"Serves you right." She held out her hand to Esteban and smiled. "Well, we're off to the world of honeymooners."

"I hope you have a wonderful time." He kissed her on either cheek. "Excuse me while I speak with my brother."

Anna watched him walk toward Marcos, and Hayley watched her watching him.

"Well, well, well," she said provocatively.

Anna looked at her cousin. "Well, well, well, what?"

Hayley inclined her head toward Esteban.

"Oh."

"Oh? The look in your eyes says a lot more than simply 'oh.'"

"He's a very attractive man."

"I've noticed. So has every other woman here. It runs in the Alvarado family." She looked at Anna. "I must say, the two of you seem to be getting along quite well."

"We are," Anna said matter-of-factly.

"Then why do you sound less than pleased?"

"I wasn't aware that I did."

"Now you are."

"Hayley, you're reading things into my tone that I never intended."

Hayley looked at her closely, then sighed. "I'm sorry. Chalk it up to wishful thinking."

"Well, cut it out. I'm not in the market."

"You just think you're not."

Anna rolled her eyes.

"All right, all right," Hayley said, raising her hands in surrender. "Consider the subject closed."

"Until the next time it comes up."

"Exactly."

Anna laughed and hugged her cousin. "Despite everything, I've really missed you. Call me as soon as you get settled in Spain, so we can have a long, long talk."

"I will. And you're going to have to come for a visit. I want you to see my new home."

Marcos signaled to Hayley, who in turn squeezed Anna's hand. "This is it. I'm off to start my new life."

"And it's going to be a wonderful one." Anna hugged her tightly. "Talk to you soon."

She watched as the two of them started to leave, but Hayley stopped suddenly and raised her hand. "Wait! I forgot something." She picked up her bouquet from a nearby table and carried it to Anna, placing it securely in her cousin's arms. "I know the custom is to throw it, but I knew exactly where I wanted it to land and I'm not taking any chances. Use it well."

Esteban was suddenly beside her as they watched the couple leave. "Nice catch."

She looked up at him and smiled. "I was a whiz at bouquet-catching in junior high school. I was always the first one picked when we had teams."

"I bet you're a whiz at a lot of things." The orchestra had started playing again, and people were dancing. "Come here."

Anna hesitated.

"Why do you do that?" he asked curiously.

"What?"

"Look as though you aren't sure what to do whenever I ask you to come closer to me."

"Perhaps because I'm not sure what to do, whenever you ask me to come closer to you."

Esteban stepped in front of her, raised both of her arms to encircle his neck and put his hands at her slender waist. "This isn't so bad is it?" he asked close to her ear as their bodies began to move rhythmically to the music.

Anna trembled and his strong arms tightened around her.

"You always do that, too," he added.

This time she didn't ask him what he meant.

They danced slowly and in silence for a long time. Anna felt the strength of the shoulder under her palm and the warmth of the hand at her waist.

"Anna," he said, his mouth closer to her ear. "I want to spend some time with you before I go back to Spain."

Anna leaned back in his arms and gazed up at him as they continued dancing. "No," she said softly, her eyes on his in the light of a nearby hanging lamp.

"Why not?"

"I don't think it's a good idea."

"That doesn't answer my question."

She stopped dancing. "No, I guess it doesn't." Her hands fell to her sides, one of them still holding the bouquet. "I'm very tired, and I'm going to bed now. Good night."

Turning away from him, she made her way to her aunt and uncle to thank them and say good night, then went into the house and to her room. Without turning on the lights, Anna kicked off her shoes, peeled off her stockings and then tried to get out of the dress. She got the zipper part of the way down and it stuck in the same spot it had earlier. Anna groaned. She didn't have the energy to work with it. She was going to have to sleep in the dress.

Just as she was about to lie down, there was a knock on her door. Anna padded barefoot across the room and opened it to find Esteban standing there. Without saying anything, he put his hands on her shoulders, turned her around and unzipped her dress. "Good night, Anna."

By the time she'd turned back around, he was already on his way down the hall. Quietly thoughtful, she closed the door and let the dress slip to the floor. Taking a thin cotton nightgown from the dresser where she kept some things between visits, she slid it over her arms and head, enjoying the cool softness as it touched her skin. When she finally sank onto the bed, her entire body responded with a sigh.

Esteban Alvarado, she thought sleepily. He was interesting, but she was a little wary of him.

Her eyelids grew heavy. After a time, the music coming in through her window didn't even penetrate her sleepy haze. Within minutes she was sound asleep.

Chapter Two

Anna put her bathing suit on under slim-fitting jeans and an oversize white summer sweater the next morning. Brushing her hair back into a silky curve that touched her shoulders, she fluffed the light fringe of bangs over her forehead, took a final look at herself in the mirror and left her room only to find her father walking toward her in the hallway.

He smiled as soon as he saw her. "Oh, good. You're up. Get that file on Domenici and we can go over it now."

Anna looked at her watch. "I was just going to have some breakfast."

"You can go later. I want to get this done."

"All right. I'll get the file and meet you in the study."

Anna went back to her room and picked up her briefcase, then headed downstairs. Esteban, standing at the bottom of the stairs, fastened his gaze on her briefcase. "Work? On a Sunday?"

She stopped, her hand resting lightly on the banister, aware of the beating of her heart. She was annoyed with herself for feeling breathless and waited a moment before answering, so that he wouldn't hear it in her voice. "Just for a little while."

His eyes met hers. "Do you spend a lot of your time working, Anna?"

"Almost all of it."

"And how much time do you spend playing?"

"Not much."

"That's not healthy."

"Even if it's by choice?"

"Even so. How long are you going to be occupied with business today?"

"An hour."

"All right. Meet me on the beach in an hour."

"It might take longer."

"I'll wait."

"A lot longer."

"Then I'll wait longer. Or at least until I have to leave to catch my plane back to Spain in a few hours."

Anna smiled. "All right. I'll see you when I see you."

Esteban stepped aside and she went past him to the study.

Her father was sitting on the couch talking to Hayley's father.

"Hello, Uncle. Have you recovered from yesterday?" Anna asked him.

He rose and pinched her cheek. "I don't think I'll ever recover, Annie. Well, you two do what you have to, and," he said turning to her father, "we'll talk some more about that little matter later, Charles."

Anna sat on the couch, set her briefcase on the cushion next to her and took out a handful of files. When she got to the one labeled Domenici, she handed it to her father. "As you'll see when you study the paperwork," she said, "he really isn't in a situation where he has to sell. Your lawyer was wrong about that. He's decided how much money he wants from his stock, and to be quite honest about it, Dad, I think that if you won't agree to pay what he wants, he won't sell it to you."

She fell silent while her father read.

"What do you think?" he asked about half an hour later, when he'd finished.

"You don't need the company. If I were you, I'd pass. He's asking for more than the stock is worth, and in the end you're going to lose money on the deal."

He tossed the file onto the coffee table. "Nice work. As it happens, I agree."

"Good. I'll call him on Monday." Anna picked up the file and put it into her briefcase. "Is there anything else?"

"Just one thing. I want you in Paris on Tuesday to meet with our new corporate attorney."

Anna pulled out her calendar and flipped to Tuesday. "That means I'll have to cancel the factory tour."

"Then cancel it. You and Bill are going to be working closely together on several projects that are in the offing, and it's important for the two of you to touch base often and in depth."

"Bill Ferris," she said quietly, as she noted the name on her calendar.

"What do you think of him?"

Anna shrugged. "He seems competent."

"That's not what I meant. What do you think of the man as a person?"

A picture of the young, very handsome and intense attorney flashed into her mind. "I suppose he's nice enough."

"You suppose?"

"I've only met him once. I guess I don't really have an opinion." She put the book back in her briefcase. "Now, is that all?"

"What's your hurry?"

"I have, for lack of a better word, a date."

"With anyone I know?" he asked, already knowing the answer.

"The odious Dr. Alvarado," she said with a lowered voice and a twinkle in her eye.

Her father had the grace to tinge his smile with embarrassment. "All right, I admit I'm not crazy about the man."

"Then it's a good thing that I have the date with him rather than you." She started to rise from the couch, but her father reached across the coffee table and caught her hand to keep her seated. Anna looked into her father's worried eyes and her teasing manner turned serious. "What's wrong?"

"I told you last night. I don't like the man. There's something about him that makes me nervous."

Anna sighed.

Her father leaned toward her. "Anna, you're my only child; my only heir. All that I've accomplished over the years in building this business, I've done for you. You've tailored your education toward some day taking over, and I don't want to see you get side-tracked by some smooth-talking Casanova."

It was the first time Anna had ever heard her father sound insecure, and it touched her heart. "Dad," she said gently, "have I ever let you down before?"

"No. You've never been anything but a joy to me."

"And I won't let you down now. I know what my responsibilities are, believe me, both to you and to the company."

He reached across the table and squeezed her hand. "I know you would never intentionally disappoint me."

"Then stop worrying. I'm hopelessly levelheaded. You know that."

"So I do," he said with a small smile. "It would seem that I've raised you well."

"Thank you for that acknowledgement. And now, if you don't mind, I'm going to meet Esteban Alvarado on the beach for a short time before he goes back to Spain."

"He's going back to Spain today?"

"That's right."

"Good."

Anna rose, leaned over and kissed the top of her father's head. "Don't worry about me so much." Leaving her briefcase in the study, she left the room and closed the door behind her, then stood there lost in thought.

"Hello, dear," her uncle said as he rounded a corner. "All finished with business?"

"Yes."

"Is your dad still in there?"

"Umm-hmm."

He walked past her into the study. Anna stood there for a moment longer, then headed out of the cool house into the warm sunlight. Standing on the patio, she let herself adjust to the brightness. Esteban was standing near the cliff with his back to her. Even from this distance his was a commanding presence, in shorts that exposed his long, strong legs, and a knit shirt that stretched tautly over his broad shoulders. As though sensing her presence, he turned and looked at her.

Anna studied him a moment longer before crossing the lawn toward him.

"What's wrong?" he asked, as his eyes carefully examined her face.

She squinted in the sunlight as she looked up at him, in genuine surprise. "What makes you think something's wrong?"

"You're very pale."

"Oh," she said with a smile, "that's because I haven't seen the sun for a while."

Esteban wasn't convinced, but he let it pass. Taking her arm, he helped her down the steps. They crossed the sand toward her favorite rock. A blanket was spread on the sand and a picnic basket sat waiting.

"A picnic? For breakfast?" she asked delightedly, as she sat cross-legged on the blanket and opened the basket. "What a wonderful idea."

Esteban stretched casually out on the blanket, propping himself up on an elbow, and watched her. "Go ahead and unpack it, if you'd like."

"I would. I'm starving." Layer by layer, she made her way to the bottom of the basket as she removed plates and napkins, glasses, orange juice, silverware, jam and honey, croissants and thin slices of ham. "What would you like?" she asked.

"Anything you give me."

She put a little of everything on his plate and poured him a glass of juice, then did the same for herself.

From the corner of her eye, Anna watched as Esteban picked up his juice, tilted his head back exposing his strong throat, and drank until the juice was gone. Setting the empty glass on the blanket, he picked up his croissant and eyed Anna. "Tell me about yourself, Anna Bennett. Where's your home?"

She nibbled her own croissant. "I don't really have a permanent place. Mostly I go from hotel to hotel."

"That's a rather nomadic life. Don't you ever get tired of it?"

"Not really. It's what I'm used to. My mother died when I was four, and I've traveled with my father ever since."

"And he's never had a permanent home?"

"Just hotels. Even in Paris where we have our corporate headquarters, we live in a hotel. It keeps life interesting." A smile touched her mouth, as she looked out at the ocean. "But even though I wouldn't change things, I think the reason I love coming here so much is that it's something constant in my life. This place, and my aunt and uncle and Hayley."

"Are they your only family besides your father?"

Anna nodded. "I hope you get a chance to know them. They're wonderful people."

"You seem very fond of them."

"Oh, I am. My aunt and uncle are as close to me as parents, and Hayley is more like a sister than a cousin."

"So I gathered. What about your education? Didn't it suffer with all of the traveling?"

"Not at all. Tutors came with us until after high school, then I went to Europe for college."

"Did you graduate?"

"When I was eighteen."

"A prodigy, no less."

Anna grinned. "I wish I could say that was true. My father certainly liked to think so. But those of us in the know attribute it to intensive tutoring."

Esteban smiled also. "And then what? Did you go to work for your father?"

She nodded. "Six years ago, right out of college."

"That's all very pat. Did you ever consider taking another course?"

"Such as?"

"I don't know," he said with a shrug. "Joining the Peace Corps."

Anna smiled. "No. My course has been charted for as long as I can remember. Right now I'm what you might call my father's apprentice. When he's ready to retire, I'll take over Bennett Industries."

"What about what you want?"

She looked at him in surprise. "That's what I want, too, of course."

"Of course." He didn't seem convinced.

"It is." Anna wasn't at all defensive. Just very sure of herself. "I love the company and I love the work. There isn't anything I'd rather do."

Esteban's gaze roamed over Anna. Her shining hair fell like sunlight around her lovely face. Her eyes had a crystalline clarity that he'd never seen before, and she had a direct way of looking at him that he found intriguing.

Anna's eyes met his. "You're staring at me."

"Yes, I know."

She was almost smiling, but not quite. "Stop it."

"You should be used to being looked at."

"I am, but not like that."

"Like what?"

"An after-breakfast snack."

"That's a novel way of putting it."

"I'm nothing if not novel."

"I've noticed."

Her gaze dropped.

"Tell me something, Anna. Why does your father dislike me so much?"

She nearly choked on her croissant. "Does he?"

"Don't play innocent. It doesn't suit you."

"Sorry. I was trying to spare your feelings."

"If I'd wanted my feelings spared, I wouldn't have asked the question. Why doesn't your father like me?"

"It isn't that he doesn't like you precisely. I think it's more that he's afraid of you."

"Because of you?"

Anna tilted her head slightly as she looked at him. "Yes. How did you know?"

"He's very possessive of you."

"Not really. At least not in the sense you're implying."

"In what sense, then?"

"He lives in fear that I'll fall in love with the wrong man, get married and desert him."

"And in his eyes, I'm the wrong man."

"Oh, yes, very definitely."

"Because?"

"He wants me to settle down with someone involved in Bennett Industries, and rightly so. The business is a huge part of my life already, and is only going to become an even larger part when I take it over completely. If I choose to marry at some point, the most logical person would be someone with a similar interest. Otherwise the marriage will be over before it starts."

"And do you always do the logical thing?"

"Always."

"So unlike your father, you have no fear that you'll fall in love with the wrong man."

"None. I won't allow it to happen."

"And what if a man were to set out with great determination to seduce you, Anna Bennett?"

Her eyes met his. "Oh, I'm human. I might well be seduced physically, but never emotionally."

Esteban lightly touched her cheek. "Watch yourself carefully. Things happen to us at times that we don't plan on and have no control over."

"I'll consider myself warned," she said, not taking him seriously. "Now, that's enough about me. I'd like to know more about you." She looked up again. "What kind of doctor are you?"

"In America, I think you'd call me a general practitioner."

"Do you have a large practice?"

"That depends on what one's idea of large is. I take care of the people on my ranch and in the village."

"Why?"

He lifted a dark brow. "Why?"

Anna smiled disarmingly. "I didn't mean that the way it sounded. It's just that most of the doctors I know who come from small towns end up with practices in large cities. Financially speaking, it's much more rewarding."

"I didn't become a doctor to get rich. The cities have all the doctors they need. The village has only one, and before I was there it had none."

Anna warmed toward him, and it showed in her eyes.

A slow smile curved Esteban's mouth. "Don't tell me you've decided to like me, now that I've confessed to being poor."

She smiled also. "I've never met a man like you. Most of the people I know are concerned only with the bottom line. You don't even care if there is a bottom line."

"Oh, I care. There are lots of things I could do with money. But everyone has to make a choice in his or her life, and what I'm doing is my choice."

Anna nibbled her croissant. "Hayley told me a little about your ranch. She said that you and Marcos run it together. What exactly do you raise?"

"Cattle and horses, mostly. We also breed some bulls, but not many."

"How large a ranch is it?"

"About seven hundred square miles."

"Is it a kind of generational proposition?"

"Generational proposition? I don't understand."

"I mean, is it something that's been in your family for a long time?"

"Oh. You could say that. The first Alvarado took up residence on it in 1549."

Anna looked at him in amazement. "I can't even imagine being a part of a tradition that old."

"That's quite a normal thing in Spanish families. Particularly those in Andalusia."

"I understand that your ranch is very isolated."

"Hayley again?"

Anna nodded.

"She seems to have told you quite a lot."

"We talk about almost everything. Especially lately. She's been so nervous. It wasn't just that she was getting married, but she's moving to Spain and taking up a way of life she's never experienced before."

"I see. Well, she's right. We are isolated, but personally that's something I've always loved about our home."

"I'm sure she will, too, once she gets used to it."

"Time alone will tell. What about you, Anna? Could you ever get used to the isolation?"

She thought about it for a moment, then shook her head. "I doubt it."

Esteban studied her lovely face. "I do, too."

She turned her head and met his look. "I think I'm insulted."

"Don't be. I could never get used to your world of telephones and computers and constant travel."

"So we're even."

"So it would appear." He looked at her for a moment longer, then rose. "I'm going swimming. Do you want to come?"

Anna shaded her eyes from the bright sun as she looked up at him. "Not just yet."

She watched as he took off his shirt, her eyes moving unself-consciously over his strong, dark body. His arms and shoulders were beautifully muscled, his stomach flat and ridged. It was more like the body of a rancher than a doctor.

Her gaze followed him as he crossed the sand and dove into the surf. He powerfully stroked his way through the water until he was no more than a distant speck on the horizon, then started back. Anna put the breakfast things back into the basket, then rose and stripped down to her one-piece black bathing suit, folded her clothes into a neat pile beside the blanket and lay on her back with her eyes closed, soaking up the warmth of the sun. She lay there for a long time, deliberately not letting herself think about the man in the water. The very *attractive* man in the water.

At first the sun felt good against her skin, but then it got a little too warm, and the more she listened to the water, the more she wanted to be in it. Sitting up,

Anna spotted Esteban in the distance. Running gingerly across the hot sand, she splashed into the surf and gracefully dove under. She surfaced a moment later, and began swimming out to Esteban.

Esteban had been swimming laps. He'd stopped for a moment and was treading water when he spotted Anna. At about the same time he saw a flash of light from the corner of his eye. Raising his head, he saw a boat skimming across the water at a tremendous speed and making remarkably little noise. It was following a straight path, parallel to the beach. He looked at Anna and his heart moved into his throat. She was swimming right into its path, completely unaware of its presence. He didn't even bother to yell. If Anna didn't hear the boat, she probably wouldn't hear him. Swimming faster than ever before in his life, Esteban flew through the water. His muscles strained to their limit, but he didn't notice. His entire focus was on getting to Anna.

Anna lifted her head. Her ears were plugged with water, so she didn't really hear anything, but she felt a strange vibration. When she shook her head to clear the water out of her ears she heard the sound of a motorboat close by and turned her head to see where it was. Anna froze.

"Dive!"

Esteban's shout brought Anna back to her senses, but before she could get her body to move he shoved her under the water, pushing her down hard and propelling himself after her, forcing her further and further down. Almost immediately the bottom of the boat flashed by above them, its dangerous propellors churning the water wildly.

With his hands under her arms, Esteban pulled her to the surface with him. As soon as her head broke the surface, Anna desperately pulled air into her lungs, choking on it even as she breathed. Esteban held her firmly in his arms. "My God," he said, breathing hard, "are you all right, Anna?"

She nodded, still gasping for air. "I can't believe how close that boat came! If you hadn't pushed me under..." Her words trailed off as she became aware that every time she took a breath her breasts, with nipples hardened by the cold water, pressed against Esteban's bare chest.

He felt it, too. His tawny eyes moved over her face. "Your heart's pounding."

Her eyes were locked with his. She moved her hand between their bodies and rested the palm against his chest. "So's yours."

They each treaded water as their bodies were held suspended, their legs brushing against each other. Esteban's black hair was slicked straight back.

He moved his hands to her hips, pulling her body even closer against his until all that separated them were the thin shields of wet, smooth nylon. Their lips were only inches apart. The muscle in his jaw tightened.

Anna felt him move against her, and inhaled sharply as she closed her eyes. Her body filled with a delicious warmth.

Esteban raised a hand to push her wet hair behind her ear as she opened her eyes and looked into his.

Suddenly he let go of her and they drifted apart. The cold water rushed between them. In silence, they swam to shore and crossed the sand to where they'd left their things. Both pulled on their clothes without bothering to towel off the water. Neither looked at the other, but each was very much aware.

Anna helped him fold the blanket and draped it over her arm while Esteban picked up the basket. Crossing the beach again, they climbed the stairs and walked to the house.

"Anna!" her aunt said as soon as she saw them. "There you are. Your father's been looking all over for you."

"Did he say what he wanted?"

"Something about business, dear, I'm sure. It always is. He's in the study."

"Thank you."

"Of course." The older woman smiled pleasantly at Esteban before walking past them and out the door.

Anna, feeling suddenly shy and trying hard not to show it, straightened her shoulders and turned to Esteban with a smile. "Thank you for the nice picnic and the timely rescue."

Esteban's eyes moved over her face with such dark intensity that it took her breath away. "I'm leaving in an hour, Anna."

His words caught her unaware. "I see."

Cupping her chin in the palm of his hand, his gaze moved over her face, feature by feature. "Goodbye," he finally said softly, his hand dropping to his side.

Anna watched him walk away from her, wanting him to stay and yet relieved that he was leaving, all at the same time.

"Anna," her father said as he walked up behind her.

She gasped and turned to him. "You startled me."

"Sorry. Something's come up. I need you to fly to London to handle it."

"When?"

"Right away."

She turned to her father and pushed Esteban from her mind. That was the wonderful thing about business. She could lose herself in it....

Chapter Three

A year later Anna paced the length of the sitting room of her hotel suite. She was so restless. Nothing she did put her at ease. The more she threw herself into her work, the more restless she became.

Stopping in front of her window, Anna stared across the Tokyo skyline. She crossed her arms over her breasts and rubbed her hands up and down her arms.

"Here are those letters you wanted typed," said her secretary as she walked into the suite.

Anna turned with a halfhearted smile. "Thanks, Gail."

"And I have some phone messages for you."

Anna took the stack of messages and flipped negligently through them until she got to one with Hayley's name on it.

"Did my cousin say what she wanted?"

"Only that she needed to talk with you."

Anna sat on the couch and read through the letters, leaning forward to sign each one on the coffee table when she was through. "Here," she said as she handed them back to her secretary. "Anything else?"

"Your father called, also. He wants you to stay in Tokyo for another week."

Anna leaned back against the couch and sighed.

"Don't you want to?"

"I don't know what I want." She was lost in her own thoughts, but just for a moment. Looking up at her secretary, she smiled. "It's late and you've put in a hard day. Why don't you go out and try to enjoy what's left of the evening?"

Gail grinned. "Thank you. I'll do my best. And if I might be so bold, I'd recommend the same for you."

The phone rang and Gail picked it up on the second ring, spoke for a moment, then held it out toward Anna. "It's your fiancé."

"He's not my fiancé *yet*," Anna said with quiet amusement as she took the phone.

"As persistent as he is, it won't be much longer." Gail turned and waved cheerfully over her shoulder as she left the suite.

Anna waited until the door had closed behind her secretary before speaking into the receiver. "Hello, Bill."

"Hello, darling. How are you?"

"Just fine."

"I spoke with your father earlier this afternoon. He said you were going to be in Tokyo a little longer."

"Another week, according to Gail."

"Another long week. You know why I'm calling, don't you?"

"I'm afraid I do."

"Are you going to have an answer for me when you get to New York?"

"I told you that I need time..."

"You've had a month already."

"That's not enough, Bill. This is one of the biggest decisions of my life."

"I know, and I don't mean to push you, but I want us to be together."

"I'm sorry. I know I'm handling this badly."

"We make a wonderful corporate team."

"Yes, we do."

"Your father's given me his wholehearted approval."

"I know he has."

There was a pause. "Look, Anna, I know you're not wildly in love with me, but try to look at what we do have."

"I've been doing that."

"We have the same goals, the same interests. We lead similar lives and we're both completely dedicated to Bennett Industries. Am I right?"

"Yes."

"So while you're thinking about us, think about that."

"I will."

"I'll call again tomorrow."

"Okay. But I'm still not going to have an answer."

"I'll try to be patient."

Anna smiled. She might not be in love with him yet, but she was definitely fond of him. "Goodbye."

"Goodbye, darling."

No sooner had Anna hung up than the phone rang again.

"Anna! I can't believe how hard it is to get hold of you," a voice on the other end of the phone line said after Anna answered.

"Hayley? Hello! I was going to call you, honestly. How are you?"

"More importantly, how are you?"

"I'm fine. Why?"

"Just a feeling I've had recently. Are you sure everything's all right?"

"Quite. Now, to get back to my original question, how are you?"

"Very pregnant and a little depressed, frankly."

Anna smiled. "Just think about the end result. It'll be worth everything you're suffering now."

"That's what everyone keeps telling me." She paused for a moment. "Anna, may I ask you for a favor?"

"Anything."

"Anything?"

"Anything."

"I was hoping you'd say that. I want you to come to Spain for a visit. A long visit."

"I'd love to, Hayley, but this is a really bad time for me."

"It was a bad time for you the last time I asked."

"I know. Business has really been hectic."

"Anna, please. Couldn't you just come for two weeks? It would mean so much to me."

"I don't see how I could possibly get away."

"Oh." There was a world of sadness in that one word. "So you won't come?"

"I..."

"It's all right. I understand."

A corner of Anna's mouth lifted. "Are you trying to make me feel guilty?"

"That depends. Is it working?"

"Extremely well."

"Then you'll come?"

She shook her head in resignation. "I'll find a way to get the time off. Just let me finish up some business here and I'll be on my way."

"Promise?"

"I promise."

"You won't back out at the last minute?"

"I won't."

Hayley sighed. "I'm feeling happier already."

"Good. Is there anything I can bring for you?"

"Just yourself and a smiling face."

"I think I can manage that."

"Let me know when you'll be arriving and I'll make arrangements to have you met at the airport."

"All right. I'll call you back tomorrow."

"Anna?"

"Umm?"

"Thanks."

Anna smiled. "You're welcome."

As soon as she'd hung up, she leaned back on the couch and stared at the wall across from her. It was strange. She wanted to see Hayley, but she didn't want to go to Spain. Why? Because she didn't want to see Esteban Alvarado again. Something deep within told Anna that it would be a mistake.

But how could she not go when Hayley needed her?

She rubbed her forehead and sighed. It was probably just that her father's edginess about the man had rubbed off on her. Besides, for her to be afraid of Esteban was ridiculous. She was the master of her own fate, no one else.

Anna stepped off the propeller plane that had brought her from Madrid to this much smaller airport in southern Spain and crossed the tarmac to the terminal. As soon as she stepped inside, she saw Esteban. He didn't wave. He didn't do anything but stand there and look at her.

She stumbled in surprise, but regained her balance immediately and threaded her way through the people toward him. When she was finally standing in front of him, his eyes moved slowly over her face. "Hello, Anna."

"Hello. I wasn't expecting to see you here."

"Marcos was busy and I wouldn't let Hayley make the trip. It's a difficult drive over some very rough roads."

"Of course. I didn't realize."

"Have you ever been in Andalusia before?"

"No, but I've heard it's beautiful."

He took her carry-on case away from her and shouldered it, then put his hand under her arm as they walked to the baggage-claim area. "It is. I think it's the most beautiful part of Spain, but I'm perhaps prejudiced. I've lived here all of my life, except for when I underwent my medical training."

"I'm looking forward to seeing it."

Her luggage arrived not long after they did. There was no need to clear customs because she'd done that in Madrid, so they simply walked outside into the hot, still air toward a rickety-looking pickup truck.

"This is yours?" she asked, trying not to sound as dismayed as she felt.

Esteban put her things into the open rear, then opened the door for her. "Yes."

Anna bid a silent farewell to the white linen suit she was wearing and climbed inside.

Esteban looked at her as though he was expecting a comment. "Is everything all right?" It was as though he was challenging her to complain. Daring her.

Anna smiled innocently right into his eyes. "Everything is just fine."

With a half smile, Esteban closed her door and climbed into the driver's side. The engine struggled to start, but caught on the third or fourth try. He moved the spindly stick shift that stuck out of the floor in front of the bench seat into gear and pulled into the light flow of traffic.

"How far is it from here to your home?"

"Do you want it in miles or kilometers?"

"Miles."

"About a hundred and fifty."

Anna mentally calculated a three-hour drive.

"Do you know anything of the history of Andalusia?" Esteban asked.

"No, I can't say that I do." She lifted her hair away from her already damp neck. "I vaguely remember something about it being occupied by the Moors at one point."

"It was, for about eight hundred years. That's why so much of the architecture here is in the Moorish style."

"I imagine that a lot of the people here are in the Moorish style, as well."

A smile curved his mouth. "Yes."

"Are you?" she asked as she glanced at him sideways, taking in the raven-black hair and dark skin. "Descended from the Moors, I mean."

"Yes. Or at least our family history would have us believe that's the case."

They had entered a main highway from the airport, but not long after, Esteban left the highway to drive along a much narrower, poorly maintained road that was composed more of loose gravel than pavement. They slowed to about half their earlier speed, and even that proved bone-jarring. After one particularly bad bounce that left Anna clinging to the dashboard in self-defense, she looked at Esteban. "Is this an original Moorish road?" she asked dryly.

Esteban laughed. "It feels like it. I wish I could say that it gets better, but it doesn't."

Anna groaned. Her entire body was going to be one big bruise. "Would there, by any chance, be a lovely ocean view at the end of this drive?"

"I'm afraid not. My ranch is inland. It's not glamorous, but just as beautiful in its own way, I think."

She had to admit that the sheer ruggedness of the land had enormous appeal. And it was ever-changing. Parts were green and full of life and parts were brown and dry. There were well-ordered fields of vines and olive trees and orange trees, and there were areas that were nothing more than dirt. The one constant was the mountains, ever present in the distance, towering over the countryside.

Esteban noticed her interest. "Those are the Sierra Nevadas," he told her.

Her gaze moved over their jagged peaks, some hidden in the clouds, in something close to awe.

As they rounded a bend in the road, Esteban slammed on his brakes, putting his arm protectively in front of Anna to keep her from hitting the dashboard. Several cows were walking slowly down the middle of the road, their bony hips swaying, followed by an old man with a switch in his hand. When he saw the truck, he waved in greeting and slowly moved the cattle to the side of the road so they could pass.

Esteban drove the truck carefully past the cows and picked up speed again.

A tiny village sprang out of nowhere, bright white in the hot sun; so white that it almost hurt to look at it. The old truck rumbled through the center of the village, down the narrow road, past other old trucks and carts pulled by donkeys. There was a village square with a large well in the center. Three women, each filling clay jugs with water, talked as they worked.

"What do you think?" Esteban asked as he looked at her.

"I feel as though I've stepped back in time."

"You have."

It took them all of four minutes to cross through the village, then they were on the road again, going downhill, raising a trail of dust behind them. Anna leaned closer to her open window and let the wind blow her hair away from her perspiring face. She didn't even bother to ask if the truck had air-conditioning.

After another hour and a half of traveling, Anna hadn't seen any further signs of civilization. That little village had been it, except for the occasional person on a donkey or a very rare car passing.

Her linen suit had given up all pretense of crispness and hung on her, limp, damp and wrinkled beyond repair. Her hair, silky and bouncy on her arrival in Spain, now clung in damp tendrils to her neck.

"I think I asked the wrong question earlier about how far away your home was. I should have asked how long it was going to take us to get there."

"Seven hours, give or take an hour. It depends a lot on the weather."

Anna looked at him in amazement. "Seven hours?"

"I told you, it's rough country. It isn't that the distance is so great. It's more that it's difficult to get from one point to another."

"Apparently." She turned in her seat so she could look at him more easily. "Do you realize that by the end of the day you will have spent fourteen hours in this heat, just to pick me up at the airport?"

A corner of his mouth lifted. "I spend all of my days in this heat. I was born in it. It seems so intense to you because you've never experienced it before today."

Anna shook her head. "I don't see how anyone—or anything—can live in it."

"You'll get used to it."

"Has Hayley?"

"Some days are better than others for her. Being pregnant makes it more difficult. Being homesick makes it more difficult, still."

There was a loud bang and the truck swerved sharply to the right, throwing Anna against the door.

Esteban swore in Spanish under his breath as he struggled with the antiquated steering system to bring the truck under control. It went off the side and slid along the gravel, finally coming to a stop half on and half off the road. The first thing Esteban did was look at Anna. "Are you all right?"

"I'm fine," she said, rubbing her bruised shoulder. "What happened?"

"A flat tire, I think." He left the truck and walked around to the rear passenger side.

Anna leaned out the window. "Is it?"

"I'm afraid so."

"What do we do now?"

Esteban had gone to the back of the truck. She heard him shifting some things around. "Well," he said as he came to her window, "ordinarily we'd change the tire."

"Ordinarily? That sounds ominous."

"It seems that Marcos forgot to put a spare in the back last week after he got a flat."

"What do we do now?"

His eyes met hers. "We walk."

Anna looked at him for a long moment, not believing what she was hearing. "You can't be serious."

"Oh, but I am."

"I couldn't possibly."

"If you have a better suggestion, I'm perfectly willing to listen."

She thought for a moment. "I don't suppose there's an auto club of some sort?"

Esteban smiled. "No."

Anna thought some more. "We could wait for another car to pass by."

"It could be tomorrow before that happens."

"All right. I've got it. We could find a telephone and call for help."

Esteban lifted an expressive brow. "Do you see any telephone lines?"

Anna looked at the clean landscape and her heart sank. "No buried cable?"

"I'm afraid not. Oh, there are some phones, to be sure. I have one at home. But they're few and far between out here. Many of the things you consider necessities, we consider luxuries."

"Oh."

"Any other suggestions?"

"We could walk, I suppose."

"Why, Anna, I wish I'd thought of that." He opened the door for her.

"That's why I get paid the big bucks." There was a disarming twinkle in her eyes as she put her hand in his and stepped down from the truck. "Now for the next problem. How are we going to carry all of my luggage?"

"We aren't."

"But..."

"Let me rephrase that. I'm not. If you'd like to give it a try, you're certainly welcome."

She walked around to the back of the truck and looked at the heavy pieces. There was no way in the world she could handle even one of them on her own. But she had to have her carry on bag. Lifting it from the rear, she slipped the strap over her shoulder. It wasn't all that heavy. "What's going to happen to the rest of it?" she asked as she went back to where Esteban was standing.

"We'll leave it here. Whoever comes to fix the truck can bring it to the house later." He looked down at her high heels. "Don't you have anything a little more practical than those?"

Anna looked at them, too. "In my world, these *are* practical shoes."

He shook his head. "I've really got to do something about bringing you into the real world while you're in Spain."

"My world is quite real enough just the way it is, thank you anyway." She hefted the bag higher onto her shoulder. "Are you ready?"

His mouth twitched. "After you."

The two of them started down the dusty, rutted road in the searing heat. Anna was used to walking in high heels. She'd been doing it for years—but not under these circumstances. She managed to go for an hour before her feet started aching enough to notice and after that it was downhill all the way. It wouldn't have been nearly so bad if the road had been level, but she was constantly stepping on rocks or into holes. She'd come dangerously close to twisting her ankle a couple of times, but she refused to complain. She knew what he was thinking: that she was some spoiled, rich American woman who couldn't take a little adversity. Well, she could handle anything he could throw at her.

The bag that had been so light when they'd started out grew increasingly heavy. The strap dug painfully into her shoulder. She began switching it back and forth. Perspiration streamed between her breasts and dampened her back, causing her jacket to stick to her body. "I need to stop for a moment. You can keep on walking. I'll catch up."

Esteban stopped walking and looked at her. "I'm not going to leave you behind."

Anna looked at him in exasperation. "Look, I want to take off some of my clothes and I don't want you watching me when I do it. All right?"

"Then just say so and I'll turn around."

As soon as he had his back to her, Anna took off her slip and panty hose and stuffed them into her shoulder bag. She would have loved to have been able to take off her jacket, but she wasn't wearing anything but a bra underneath. With a wince and a stifled groan, she pushed her aching feet back into her high heels. "All right," she said as she picked up her bag and shouldered it once again, "I'm ready to go on."

Esteban turned and waited until she was beside him, then started walking. He was very quiet, but there was no mistaking the fact that he was amused.

He had shortened his stride to accommodate hers, but it wasn't enough. There were times when she had to run a few steps to keep up, and he was so deeply involved in his own thoughts that he didn't notice. Her tight skirt was an uncomfortable hindrance and seemed to get tighter with every passing minute.

And then it happened. On one of her jogs to catch up with Esteban, her heel caught in a hole and snapped off of her shoe. Her ankle turned and she fell so quickly that Esteban didn't have time to catch her before she hit the ground.

He knelt beside her instantly. "Are you all right?"

Anna took the strap from her shoulder and sighed. "It's my ankle."

"What about it?" he asked as he moved lower.

"I think I twisted it."

Esteban took off her shoes and moved his hands gently over her left ankle.

Anna watched the top of his dark head. "It's the other one," she said after a minute.

He looked up and met her eyes before lifting her other ankle and moving his fingertips over it. "Why didn't you say so?"

"Because what you were doing felt so good." She leaned back against her bag with a sigh and closed her eyes. "Have you ever considered becoming a masseur?"

A corner of his mouth lifted. "Given the right circumstances, I'm actually a very good one."

Anna opened one eye and looked at him. "That's a provocative remark."

"It was intended to be." He felt around her foot and ankle for a moment longer. "I think you're all right. There's no sign of swelling."

She opened the other eye. "Oh, good," she said with a complete absence of sincerity. "I guess that means we can start walking again."

Esteban took her hands in his and pulled her to her feet. "That's exactly what it means."

Anna picked up her shoes and looked at them mournfully. "How am I going to walk in these?"

"I could snap the other heel off," he suggested.

Anna grimaced and closed her eyes tightly as she handed it to him. "Just be merciful and do it quickly."

There was a loud snap.

Anna opened her eyes. "Is it over?"

A corner of his mouth lifted. "Over and completely painless."

"Painless for you. You don't know what I paid for them."

"Nor do I want to know."

Esteban hoisted her bag onto his shoulder. "Let's go."

Anna held on to his arm while she slipped on the shoes. Her body tilted forward because of the angle of the shoes, kind of like a skier going downhill, but she had to admit that once she was able to figure out how to straighten herself, it was easier going.

Esteban seemed to get lost in his own thoughts. Sometimes he remembered she was there and slowed down, and sometimes he didn't. Anna was taking two steps to every one of his just to stay even, and with her feet hurting the way they did, that was no small matter. If she could just do something about her skirt.

But she could, couldn't she? it suddenly dawned on her. "Stop!" she called out.

He did, instantly concerned. "What's wrong? Is your ankle bothering you?"

"My ankle is fine. I just had a flash of inspiration. Do you have something sharp?"

Esteban looked at her suspiciously. "Why?"

Anna's dimple appeared irresistibly. "I'll admit that the thought crossed my mind, but you're safe for now."

He reached into a pocket and pulled out a small knife. "This should be interesting," he said as he held it out to her.

"Thank you." Anna bent over and eased the knife into the hem of her skirt, sawing downward back and forth until she'd made it through the hem. Then putting the knife between her teeth, she ripped the material upward, creating a slit in the front and exposing her long legs. "There," she said triumphantly as she removed the knife from her mouth and handed it back to a surprised Esteban. "That should help."

He sheathed the blade and pocketed the knife. "You could have just told me to slow down."

"Now I don't have to."

"Are you always this tenacious?"

"Almost." She started walking and Esteban fell into step beside her. Her strides were longer now, and he consciously shortened his a little so that they were traveling at a comfortable pace.

Anna tried to ignore the pain in her feet. Sometimes she did it by concentrating on her surroundings and sometimes she did it by counting steps. And sometimes she just gritted her teeth and was pleased if she managed to put one foot in front of the other without screaming.

"There's a stream about ten minutes from here where we can cool off and rest," Esteban said after what seemed like hours.

"All right."

He looked at her curiously. "You're taking all of this remarkably well."

"I learned a long time ago not to complain about things that can't be changed."

"Some people would interpret that as a weakness. An unwillingness to fight back."

"They'd be mistaken," she said quietly.

He looked down at her lovely, heat-flushed face and didn't doubt it. "Look to the right."

Anna did. "Trees," she said unenthusiastically.

"Ah, yes, but it's what's inside the ring of trees that should interest you."

Her eyes widened hopefully. "Do you mean the stream? Water? Real water?"

"Real water." There was a smile in his voice.

She walked as fast as her poor feet would allow as they left the road and went down a small hill. The trees were further away than they looked, but Anna persevered. Esteban took her hand to help her over the rocky areas, but finally they were there. Esteban lowered the bag to the ground and went to the edge of the water. Scooping it out with his hands, he splashed it over his face. Anna watched as it trickled down his throat and dampened what little remained dry of his shirt.

Anna took off her shoes and hobbled up to the stream. Tentatively at first, she went in up to her ankles and just stood there as the fast-rushing cold water soothed her feet. She daintily dipped her fingertips into it and dabbed it on her face, but it felt so good that she soon threw caution to the winds and scooped it up the same way Esteban had, splashing it onto her hot face and throat. Feeling Esteban's eyes on her, she turned her head and looked at him. He was indeed watching her with smiling eyes.

"What is it about me that amuses you so much?"

"Just watching you. You aren't at all the way I expected you to be under these conditions."

"All right," she conceded, "I'll admit that I'm not very dignified at the moment, but this feels much too wonderful for dignity."

"An interesting analogy."

Anna knew instantly what he was talking about. Her sun pinkened cheeks grew even pinker. "I didn't mean it that way."

"I know what you meant."

Anna's eyes locked with his for a moment. Then she turned away and moved further into the stream. It only went up to her hips, so she sank down in it until she could tilt her head back and wet her hair. "You know," she said with a sigh, "if anyone had told me a few hours ago that I would be taking a dip in a stream, fully clothed, I would have thought he was crazy." She raised herself out of the water and stepped onto the bank. Water poured from her, running down her legs from the soaked suit and puddling on the ground around her. "All right. I'm ready. What further tortures do you have in mind for me?"

"We walk some more."

"To anywhere in particular?"

"There's a small town about fifteen miles from here."

"Fifteen miles?" She couldn't mask the dread in her voice.

Esteban stepped out of the water and stood next to her. "Anna, you're not used to the heat and you're not used to the exercise. On top of that, your clothes are all wrong. I'd suggest that you stay here and wait for me to come back for you."

Anna was sorely tempted to accept—*sorely* being the operative word—but her pride wouldn't let her. Esteban expected her to fold under the physical pressure. Why that should matter to her one way or another, she didn't know, but it did.

Esteban saw the indecision in her face. "You'll be safe here, and comfortable. I won't be gone long," he said gently.

Her eyes met and held his. "You don't think I can hold up, do you?"

"Frankly, no." As soon as the words were out of his mouth, Esteban wished he could recall them.

"I see." She picked up her shoes and gingerly put them on her injured feet. "I'm ready whenever you are."

"I didn't mean it as a challenge, Anna. This isn't a contest to see who can hold out the longest. If it were, you'd lose. You're in no condition for this."

"I can take care of myself."

"I'm sure you can—in a boardroom. This is my turf. Let me take care of you this time."

"I'm going with you."

"God, you're a stubborn woman."

Anna didn't say anything.

He shook his head. It was obvious that there was no sense in arguing with her. "All right. But at least let me carry you."

"No, thank you. I'm too heavy and it's too hot. This may be your turf, but your name is Esteban, not Superman."

He gave up. "Fine. Have it your way." Esteban shouldered her bag and strode away from her.

Anna ran to catch up, silently cursing herself. He was right. She was stubborn, and it wasn't one of the things she liked about herself.

They'd been walking along the road for about half an hour when Anna heard hooves. She touched Esteban's arm and they both turned and looked down the road to find an ox-drawn cart rumbling toward them. Esteban waved his arms and the wizened, nut-brown man who was driving stopped. Esteban explained their predicament to him. The man nodded, and with an economy of words and lots of gestures, offered them a ride in the cart.

The two of them walked around to the rear. Esteban put his hands at Anna's waist and lifted her into the back of the twig-filled cart. As soon as he was settled next to her, the driver made a noise with his tongue and the ox started on its way. The cart jerked, but Esteban held Anna in place with an arm around her waist.

She turned her head and looked up at him. "I'm sorry. I don't mean to be so difficult."

His eyes rested on her face. "I am, too. This isn't how I wanted you introduced to my country."

"It's not your fault. In fact, if it weren't for my feet, I'd probably be enjoying the adventure of all of this. Speaking of which," she reached down and took off her shoes and tossed them into the cart, "it's gotten to the point where I think they're doing me more harm than good."

"Are you sure you want to do that? Have you ever in your life gone barefoot?"

"There's a first time for everything." The cart hit another big bump and sent her flying back into the twigs with Esteban. She looked at him with an amused twinkle in her eyes.

"What's so funny?" he asked with a smile, as he pulled a small stick out of her hair.

"The irony of my saying that there's a first time for everything. This entire day has been one big first."

He sat up and helped Anna up.

The wooden cart wheels managed to find every stone, every rut, every bump. The bundles of twigs beneath her were unforgiving, jabbing at her.

"Just keep in mind that it's better than walking," Esteban said, as though he knew what she was thinking.

Anna looked at him sideways.

They went over a particularly rough series of bumps. Esteban's grip on her tightened, as did hers on the cart. "You realize, of course," she said dryly, "that I'll never be able to bear children after this."

The cart hit another bump and nearly sent her into his lap. Esteban pulled her snugly against his side and held her in place. They rode in silence mile after mile, bump after bump. Anna missed nothing of the countryside, charmed despite herself. Certainly it was rugged, but it was also indescribably beautiful, touching something deep within her.

Esteban watched her face, enchanted with the emotions he saw, however fleeting. She was more articulate in her silence than most people were with entire dictionaries at their disposal.

He had to force his eyes away from her, but force them he did.

The cart stopped at a tiny crossroad. Esteban climbed off the back and helped Anna to the ground, then grabbed her bag. The man waved his switch at them and kept going.

Anna looked around. "What's here?"

"The little farm I told you about."

Without giving her any warning whatsoever, Esteban lifted her in his arms.

Anna started to struggle, but then realized that she was just too tired to make the effort. Her face was very close to his. "What are you doing?"

"Carrying you."

"So," she said softly as she looked into his tawny eyes, "it turns out that you're Superman, after all."

He started walking. "You talk too much."

"Yes," she agreed with a sigh. "Yes, I do. I'll stop instantly," she said as she put her arms around his neck and rested her head on his shoulder.

The road they were on wasn't really a road. It was more of a track. No attempt had been made at paving. Not even stones. There were simply two dirt ruts with grass growing between them. Esteban was walking down the middle where the ground was smoother.

"Now you're too quiet," he said after half an hour had passed. "What are you thinking about, Anna?"

A smile touched her mouth. "Oh, I was just mentally composing a thank-you note to the manufacturers of the deodorant I put on this morning. I can give them an incredible testimonial."

Esteban laughed out loud at her answer. "And here I was expecting something deeply intellectual."

"Not today." Anna raised her head and looked into his eyes. "You have a wonderful laugh."

At that moment, a small house came into view around a corner. Like all of the other buildings she'd seen, it was blindingly white. There was some grass, but not much, and ramshackle fences separating tiny pastures. Chickens pecked at the dirt and scattered excitedly at their approach.

There was a rickety old table, its white paint badly chipped, pushed up against the house. Esteban gently set Anna on it. "I know the people who live here. They have a mule they might be willing to loan us."

Anna tried not to look as horrified as she felt. "A mule?"

He lifted her right foot and looked at the blisters, then did the same with the left. "Don't worry about it. It's not much different than riding a horse."

"Oh, good. I mean, it would be good if I'd ever ridden a horse."

Esteban looked at her in amazement. "You can't ride?"

"No."

"I thought all rich girls rode horses."

"Not this one. If it didn't have anything to do with running a company, I didn't do it."

He shook his head. "You've really been deprived. I'll have to take care of that while you're in Spain." He walked to the door and knocked on it. No one answered.

"They're probably working in the fields." He came back to Anna, took off his shirt and ripped it into strips, then kneeling in front of her, he wound them expertly around her feet. "We'll take care of you properly when we get home."

"Tonight?"

"I don't think so. We could stay here tonight if you'd like. I'm sure we'd be welcome."

"But then it would take us longer to get home tomorrow."

"That's right."

"I think I'd rather start out tonight and get as far as we can. Hayley's going to be worried."

"Maybe a little, but she knows you're with me." He finished tying off the last strip of his shirt, straightened and held out his hand to her. "Stand up and see how that feels."

Anna put her hand in his. Very carefully, she put first one foot and then the other onto the ground. "That's much better, thank you."

A chicken who'd wandered too close to them suddenly realized that it wasn't alone and panicked. It clearly intended to run away from them, but bumped into another chicken instead and, hysterically clucking and flapping its wings, feathers flying, got turned around and crashed into Anna who in turn screamed in surprise and fell against Esteban. He caught her in his arms and held her. Her eyes met his and they both started to laugh.

And then their laughter faded. Esteban pushed her hair away from her face, cupped her cheek and rubbed his thumb over her lips. His mouth moved closer to hers.

Anna had no thought for the consequences of her actions. Her lips parted softly as she rose up on her toes....

Chapter Four

Someone called Esteban's name, but neither of them moved. Esteban was so close to her that Anna could feel his breath move her hair. Only his hands were touching her, but the heat from his body washed over her already hot skin and left it tingling. His tawny eyes were locked with hers. His body had tensed, but now it relaxed as he dropped his hands and stepped past her to greet the man walking toward them.

Anna remained with her back toward the newcomer, her hand over her pounding heart, her breathing ragged. It took her a full minute to get herself under control. After taking a deep breath and then slowly exhaling, Anna turned around, her poise in place and a polite smile curving her mouth. Esteban introduced her to the tall, lean man who owned the farm. Anna stepped forward, wobbling just a little on her bandaged feet and held out her hand, greeting him in perfect Spanish.

Esteban looked at her in surprise. "I didn't know you spoke Spanish."

"There's a lot about me you don't know," she said provocatively without looking at him.

They followed the man, Juan, to a small shed where he kept his tools. Esteban explained what had happened and asked if they could borrow his mule.

Juan was a little difficult for her to understand because of the extreme difference in pronunciation of his Andaluz Spanish and the Castilian Spanish Anna had learned, but it was clear that he wanted to help.

When they were outside once again, Juan led them to a paddock where a mule stood quietly with its ears and tail twitching at the flies.

A fly buzzed Anna's head and she shooed it away with a wave of her hand as she walked around the mule's paddock, leaving Esteban to talk to Juan. In the distance were the mountains. They didn't seem any closer than they had when she and Esteban had started their journey. Not far from the paddock was a grove of olive trees, their gnarled trunks rising out of the soil in neat rows.

But of everything that surrounded her, the thing that struck her the most was the silence. Anna had never heard anything like it. The heat suddenly wasn't so uncomfortable. It was simply there, a part of all of this.

A light breeze came out of nowhere, lifting the damp tendrils of hair from her neck and cooling her off.

Though she hadn't heard him approach, she knew that Esteban was standing behind her.

"It's beautiful, isn't it?" he asked quietly.

Her eyes moved over the miles and miles of unpopulated land. "Yes," she said simply.

"I came to tell you that the mule is ready. We should be leaving. It's going to be dark in a few hours."

Anna shook her head as she turned. "A mule. Whoever would have thought it would come to this?"

"Juan packed some food for us, too. We can eat now if you'd like."

Her eyes met his. "I'm not really hungry."

"All right."

Anna followed him back around the paddock. Juan was waiting with his mule. A blanket had been tossed over its back, but no saddle. Her case, some water bottles and a sack hung along the mule's sides, held by a rope. Esteban hoisted Anna onto its back, then raised himself up behind her. "Ready?" he asked as his arms went around her to hold the reins.

Her back rested against his bare chest. She instantly straightened away from him. "As ready as I'll ever be."

Esteban said something to Juan and then the two of them were on their way. "So tell me," he said conversationally after they'd been riding for several minutes, "how did you learn to speak such pretty Spanish?"

"Speaking different languages is more or less a necessity for me in business. I started with Spanish when I was about three and had a Spanish nanny."

"What other languages are you fluent in?"

"Italian, French and German. And I can get along in a few other languages if the conversation is kept simple."

"Your father certainly started working on you early in life, didn't he?"

"If you mean that he knew what kind of education I was going to need and made sure I got it, yes, he did."

The mule had to go up a hill. Anna was pressed against Esteban's chest, but as soon as the ground was level again, she straightened away from him.

She tried desperately not to notice that his arms were around her, or that the front of his body of necessity cupped the back of hers and that they moved together rhythmically with each step of the mule.

"Where are we now?" she asked, trying to distract herself.

"My land."

She looked at him over her shoulder. "Yours? When did that happen?"

"Just before we got to the stream."

"But the farm we were just at . . ."

"The land is mine. I let Juan and his family use it. His father used to work for mine."

"You *let* him use it, or you rent it to him?"

"In Juan's case, I let him use it. He works hard, but he would never have enough money to pay for land. In other cases, if a person can afford to pay, I rent it. I still have to pay property taxes, and every little bit helps."

Anna shook her head and sighed.

"Did I say something wrong?"

"Yes. I was hoping to discover that you were a disreputable scoundrel. It would make disliking you so much easier."

"But you don't dislike me."

"I know."

They rode in comfortable silence. Anna did finally let herself relax her body against Esteban's and watched as the sun began to set and the moon to rise.

Rather than following any kind of road, Esteban cut across the land. Only he knew where he was going and Anna refused to worry about it. They'd get to his home eventually.

He stopped about four hours after they'd begun, and about two hours after the sun had set. Sliding from the back of the mule, he held out his arms for Anna.

"Is this where we're going to spend the night?" she asked as she looked around.

"Yes. If we get an early start in the morning, we should arrive around noon."

Anna swung her leg over the mule's head and let Esteban lift her to the ground. He released her immediately and set about tethering the mule loosely to a tree so that it could graze. Taking the blanket from the back of the mule, he spread it on the ground, then unrolled another blanket that had been strapped to the mule along with one of the bottles of water and the sack of food. "Have a seat," he said, waving her on to the blanket. "Not very elegant, but it'll do for one night."

Anna sank onto it gratefully. "There are times when comfort is more important than elegance, and this is definitely one of those times."

"You're going to be sore in the morning."

"I know. Between the jarring I took in the truck, the walking, and now this," she said pointing at the mule, "there isn't a muscle in my body that isn't screaming obscenities at me."

Smiling, Esteban handed her the bottle. "Drink."

Anna did, then poured some onto her hands and cleaned her face the best she could.

Esteban handed her some bread. Anna leaned against the trunk of the tree and ate it slowly, savoring it, and looking at the moon. "You know," she said after a while, "I've never seen the moon this huge."

"When was the last time you really looked at it?"

"I don't know," she said quietly. "It seems that when I look out my windows at night, wherever it is I happen to be, all I see are other windows in other buildings. But no moon."

"For someone who's been given everything all of her life, you've missed out on quite a lot."

She turned her head and looked at the man next to her in the moonlight. "Do you really think so?"

Esteban reached out and touched her cheek. "Oh, Anna, you're half asleep."

She nodded slowly.

"Come on." He helped her to lie down, then rose, shook out the second blanket and put it over her. The night air was noticeably cool.

"What about you?" she asked sleepily.

"I'm going to stay up a little longer."

"All right. I'll see you in the morning."

"Good night, Anna," he said softly.

Within seconds she was sound asleep. Esteban stood leaning against the tree gazing down at her in the moonlight, his expression unfathomable.

Anna moved and dislodged the blanket. Esteban leaned over her to pull it back up. With a gentle hand, he pushed her hair away from her face and trailed the backs of his fingers down her smooth cheek.

When Anna awoke the next morning it was very early. The sun wasn't up completely. It took her a moment to remember where she was, but as soon as she did she looked for Esteban. Both he and the mule were gone.

She rose up on her elbows a little faster than she should have and groaned inwardly when her body protested. She was one giant ache. The pain in one muscle flowed like a river into the next, and she waited a moment before sitting up straight and looking around.

Her first impression had been right: no Esteban, no mule. Where could he have gone? With a shrug, she stood up and gingerly stretched, then folded the blankets. She wasn't really worried that he'd deserted her. He'd undoubtedly be back when he finished whatever it was he was doing.

As Anna was stacking the blankets, she heard a noise behind her. Fully expecting to see Esteban standing there, she turned with a smile that froze. Not ten feet away stood a black bull. Her heart lodged in her throat as she remained absolutely motionless, her eyes locked with the bull's. She'd seen pictures of Spanish fighting bulls. They'd always seemed so beautiful to her in a horrible kind of way. This one had a massive neck. Its horns were curved and lethal-looking.

Several moments passed before she could pull her thoughts together. There was a tree behind her. If she could just make it up that tree, the bull wouldn't be able to get at her.

Nervously licking her lips, Anna took a small, tentative step backwards.

The bull didn't move.

Emboldened, Anna took another step back.

This time the bull started toward her.

Anna turned and ran, grabbing a low limb and pulling herself up with a strength she didn't even know she had. Standing on that limb, she pulled herself up onto the next one and stood on it, clinging to the trunk and looking down at the bull, who'd come to a stop immediately beneath her.

"Oh, God, Esteban, where are you?" she breathed as she looked out across the fields.

The minutes ticked by. The bull didn't move. On the contrary. It seemed quite content to graze under the tree.

After a while, Anna wasn't so afraid. She was safe where she was. With her arms still around the trunk, she slid to a sitting position, her legs dangling over the limb.

The bull behaved as if she weren't even there.

She waved her fingers at it. "Shoo. Go away."

It kept eating.

"Oh, for heaven's sake," she said in disgust, "you go to all the trouble of chasing me up here and then you ignore me. How typically male."

She tried to think of what to do next that would keep her from being stuck in the tree indefinitely. Esteban apparently wasn't in any hurry to ride to her rescue. If she could somehow startle it into running away...

The thought became the deed, as Anna focused on a small limb to the right of her head that would make a perfect switch. Reaching up, she worked it back and forth until it snapped off in her hand. Clenching that betweeen her teeth she, with some degree of difficulty, lowered herself to the next limb, unaware of the man standing about fifty feet behind her, watching her every movement with amused tawny eyes.

Once she was securely balanced with one arm around the limb above her, Anna reached down and swung at the beast's flank with her switch. It missed. She was too far away.

Swearing softly and steadying herself by holding on to the trunk of the tree, she lowered herself into a sitting position, but didn't allow her legs to dangle this time. Her toes would have brushed the bull. With her teeth digging into her lower lip, Anna raised the switch over her head and brought it down on the bull's rump, then pulled herself back onto the higher limb to watch the fallout from a position of safety.

The bull's tail swished from side to side as though swatting at flies. He moved a step forward and continued to graze undisturbed, not even bothering to lift his great head.

Then suddenly he did lift his head, listening; alert. Esteban was walking toward him, leading the mule. To Anna's utter astonishment, he walked right up to the bull and slapped him on the rear to send him on his way. Without any kind of protest at all, the bull trotted across the field to graze about a hundred yards away. After tethering the mule, Esteban held out his arms to Anna. "You can come down now."

She stayed where she was. "I can't believe what you just did. That was a bull."

"Yes, I know."

"You walked right up to it."

"He's very old and he's never been a fighter."

Anna didn't look convinced.

"We call him Ferdinand. Does that tell you anything?"

"So he wouldn't have hurt me?"

"That's right."

"And I climbed this tree for nothing."

"And here I thought you climbed it because it was there."

Anna narrowed her eyes at him. "I wouldn't push things if I were you. I'm holding on to my sanity by a thread."

The grooves in Esteban's cheeks deepened as he held out his arms. "Come on down, Anna."

She sighed. "I feel incredibly stupid."

"Don't," he told her as he put his hands at her waist and lowered her to the ground. "You had no way of knowing. The smartest thing you could have done was go up the tree. I didn't know he was in the field, or I would have warned you before I left."

Anna tried to regain some dignity by straightening her tattered skirt. "Where did you go?"

"The mule needed some water and we needed something to eat." He handed her an orange.

She took it gratefully and dug her thumbnails into the rind. "Where did you get it?"

"From a tree."

Anna popped a section into her mouth and savored the juicy flavor that burst onto her tongue as her teeth sank into it. "Oh," she sighed, "this is delicious. I can't think of anything I'd rather eat right now."

Esteban repacked the mule. "Are you ready to face traveling again?"

"I'm not looking forward to it, but I can handle it."

Esteban lifted her onto the mule, then got on behind her. "Just a few more hours and we'll be there."

Anna looked at him over her shoulder as they started to move. "Are you angry with me?"

"No. Why?"

"Just an impression I get." Anna turned around and faced forward.

"I'm not angry, at all. I think you've just taken me off guard."

"Off guard?"

"I thought the ride in the truck was going to be difficult for you. I expected you to complain all the way to the ranch."

"Why?"

"Because you've been so pampered all of your life. I didn't think you'd be able to handle even mild discomfort."

"I see."

"And here we are, a day later, still traveling, but less conventionally; we're both dirty, sore and tired. You've walked until your feet blistered, ridden on the back of a cart, been chased up a tree and bounced on a mule, and other than the occasional wisecrack, you haven't uttered a word of complaint."

"I'm glad you noticed."

"It's been deliberate?"

"Let's just say that there are grooves in my tongue from clamping my teeth on it."

Esteban laughed, his mouth close to her ear. "And you're refreshingly honest."

Anna turned her head again and looked into his eyes for a long moment, then faced forward.

The cool air from the dawn was quickly replaced by searing heat as the sun rose in the sky. They crossed pasture after pasture, and Esteban had to climb down from the mule to open and close gates before and after they passed through them. Anna watched the muscles in his back and arms strain as he lifted the heavier gates. His skin was coated with a fine film of perspiration. When he climbed up behind her, his arms around her to hold the reins, the manly smell of him filled her senses. There was no cologne or aftershave. Just Esteban, and it was intoxicating.

There was no place to run; no chance of getting away. She was here with him, her body touching his and her imagination reeling. But that was all right—as long as she could keep things in perspective and separate fantasy from reality.

Even as she thought it, Anna felt better. She'd always prided herself on being levelheaded. It was a quality she trusted in herself.

For the first time in hours, she let herself relax.

Esteban felt the change in the way Anna leaned against him and wondered at it.

When it was almost noon, with the heat beyond belief, Esteban suddenly stopped the mule. "Look, Anna," he said softly against her ear.

Anna looked in the direction he was pointing. There on a small hill perhaps a mile away was a white hacienda, its doorways and window wells gracefully arched. The roof was covered in red tiles. It wasn't large, but it was beautiful.

Esteban pressed the mule's flanks with his knees and they started moving again, through the final field and around a low stone wall. There was a well in the middle of the yard. They rode past it and straight to the hacienda. Esteban slid to the ground, then lifted Anna down. As she stood looking around, he tethered the mule to a rail that ran along the porch.

Brightly colored flowers bloomed everywhere; all over the yard, and in window boxes and in pots that hung in the doorways.

Esteban put his hand under her elbow and guided her up the steps and into his home. The front hall had a red tile floor and white walls. The brightness of the home was offset by the heavy, dark and elaborately carved Spanish furniture.

"Anna!" Hayley yelled from the end of the hall, and she walked toward them as quickly as her pregnant bulk would allow, arms outstretched.

Anna hugged her gently. "Oh, Hayley, you look so..."

"Massively with child?" she suggested with a twinkle.

"Beautiful."

"Oh, thank you. I needed that." She stepped back and looked at the two of them. "Good grief, you two look terrible."

Anna involuntarily looked at Esteban and he looked at her. Without even realizing they were doing it, they smiled at each other.

Hayley looked interestedly at each of them in turn. "Marcos found the truck late last night. I was frantic, but he said you'd be showing up this afternoon—and here you are."

"Do you know what he did with the truck, Hayley?" Esteban asked.

"Changed the tire and brought it home. It's parked in the stables."

"Good."

"And while you were gone, one of Mrs. Carillo's children came to get you. He said his father was thrown from a horse."

"Has there been any word on Maximo?"

"He's home."

Esteban looked suddenly grim. "Thank you." He was speaking to Hayley, but looking at Anna. "I think that your cousin would probably like to go to her room and take a bath. And she could use some practical clothes and shoes to wear." Then he spoke directly to Anna. "I want to take a look at your feet after you've gotten cleaned up."

"They don't hurt nearly as much as they did yesterday."

"Good. I still want to see them."

"All right."

"Anything else I should know about, Hayley?"

"Only that Margarita and her parents are coming for dinner tonight."

"What time?"

"Nine o'clock."

"I'll try to make an appearance. Excuse me." He went past them and up the stairs.

Hayley looked at Anna and lifted an expressive brow. "So, what's going on between the two of you?"

Anna looked at her in amazement. "What makes you think anything is?"

"Just the way you behave around each other."

Anna smiled at her in affectionate exasperation. "I've been here less than five minutes and you're already trying to play matchmaker. Please don't. I'm practically an engaged woman."

"What?" Hayley asked in surprise.

"I'll tell you about it later."

"But..."

"Would you take me to my room? I can't begin to tell you how desperately I want to be clean."

Hayley looped her arm through Anna's as they started up the stairs. "It's quite obvious to me that we have a lot of catching up to do."

"A lot."

"You never mentioned anything in your letters about being almost engaged."

"I know."

"Why not?"

"Because I hadn't made up my mind yet."

"Who is this mystery man."

"Bill Ferris. You don't know him."

"Are you in love with him?"

"I'm very fond of him."

"That wasn't what I asked."

"I'm very, very fond of him."

"So you're *not* in love with him."

"Hayley," she said wearily, "later please. I'm too tired for this right now."

They reached the top of the stairs and turned to their left. Anna's room was just two doors down the hall. "Marcos and I are at the end of the hall," Hayley explained, "and Esteban is there." She pointed to the room directly across from Anna's.

"Thank you."

"And as soon as you're bathed and rested, I want an itemized account of everything you haven't seen fit to mention in your letters."

"I promise."

"And then I want a moment-by-moment description of your trip here."

"You'll be bored. Nothing happened."

"I'll take my chances. Don't be too long."

"I won't."

"Your luggage is here, but I think Esteban's right about finding you something appropriate to wear. All you ever bring anywhere are business clothes. I'll bring some of my own things down."

"Thanks."

Hayley put her hands on Anna's shoulders and kissed her cheek. "I'm really glad you came. I can't begin to tell you how lonely I've been."

Anna touched Hayley's hair, suddenly aware of a kind of sadness that she hadn't noticed before. "Are you all right?"

Her dark eyes filled with tears that she quickly dashed away. "Oh, I think I've just been pregnant for too long. I'm tired and cry at the drop of a hat. Don't pay any attention to me."

"Are you sure that's it?"

Hayley sniffed. "I'm sure."

"I'll get cleaned up and then the two of us are going to sit down and have a long, long talk."

"In English. The only people I've been able to really talk to since I got here are Marcos and Esteban."

"Are you learning Spanish?"

"I'm trying, but I'm terrible."

"It'll get easier with time."

"I know." Hayley sniffed again. "I'll get those clothes for you. Hurry up."

Anna watched curiously as her cousin disappeared down the hall into her own room. Something was wrong.

Chapter Five

Anna stood in the shower unmoving and just let the water run over her tired and aching body. After a while, she washed her hair and soaped her skin, then closed the drain and let the tub fill with clean, warm water. Sinking into it up to her chin, she lay there with her eyes closed. No bath had ever felt this good. She could have spent the rest of her life in it.

But reality called and after a while she climbed out and rubbed her skin down with clean towels that had been waiting for her in the bathroom. Her hair had already started to dry so she just brushed it out and left it alone.

Hayley had brought in some clothes and put them on the bed. Anna picked out a short white pair of culottes and a white sleeveless blouse. There was a pair of shoes alongside the bed that she knew would fit her because she and Hayley wore the same size, but Anna left her feet bare. The thought of anything touching the blisters on the soles of her feet was more than she wanted to contemplate.

Her suitcases had been set against a wall. She lifted one onto the bed and started to unpack, but then stopped. She didn't feel like unpacking. She didn't feel like doing anything but visiting with Hayley.

Leaving everything the way it was, she left her room. Esteban stepped into the hall at the same time. He'd changed into jeans and a blue-and-white striped shirt with the sleeves rolled to just below his elbows. His dark hair was still wet and slicked back. He looked at Anna and smiled, and her heart began that steady, solid beating it always did when he was near. "That's quite an improvement. You look much better than you did."

"Bathing and clean, unripped clothing tend to do that for a person."

He reached out and touched her face. "Your face got too much sun."

She stepped away from him. "It'll fade."

His hand fell to his side. "And your feet?"

"I think if I can just go barefoot for a few days they'll be fine."

"Let me see."

Anna sat in a chair in the hall while Esteban kneeled in front of her examining one foot at a time. "They're going to be fine," he said after a moment, straightening away from her and helping her to her feet. "I'll send some antiseptic to your room. Use it before you go to bed tonight."

"I will."

He looked at his watch.

"You'd better go. That man who fell off his horse is probably waiting for you."

Esteban took her arm and they walked downstairs together. "I think you'll probably find Hayley in the courtyard," he said as he led her through the house and out the doors to a sunny courtyard. Hayley was seated in the middle in the shade of a tree, reading a book.

She looked up at their approach and smiled. "Now you look more like the cousin I remember."

"Thanks for the clothes," Anna said as she sat in a comfortable lawn chair. "I'm going to have to go shopping for some casual things one of these days."

"What's the point? You'd only use them when you come here. You might as well use mine."

Esteban looked at his watch. "If you ladies will excuse me, I have to leave. If I'm delayed, make my excuses to our guests, Hayley."

"All right. And I'll make sure that your dinner is kept in the warming oven."

"Thanks." He ruffled Hayley's hair affectionately. "Don't look so sad. Before you know it the baby will be here and you'll be feeling much better."

Hayley smiled at him. "How's that?"

"An improvement."

"Oh," she sighed, "ignore me. I think I just want my waistline back. I'm amazed at how vain I am, and have probably always been without realizing it."

Esteban's eyes rested on Anna. Without saying anything else, he turned and left.

Hayley closed her book. "You certainly saw a lot more of the ranch on your first day here than I did."

"It was quite an incredible journey. I've been considering changing my name to Natty Gann."

Hayley laughed.

"It's absolutely huge."

"Oh, I know," Hayley said with a nod. "Sometimes I think it just goes on and on. It eats up all of Marcos's time."

"Perhaps. But it's his home."

"I know," she said quietly.

"And yours."

She sighed. "That's taking a little more getting used to than I expected."

Anna looked at her in surprise. "Don't you like it here, Hayley?"

"Oh, Anna," she said, her voice lowered to keep anyone from overhearing, "sometimes I think I'm going to go insane. There's no one to talk to; nothing to do. My husband is never around and when he is, he's exhausted from working."

"You never said anything about that in your letters or during our phone conversations."

"It's not an easy subject to discuss. What could I have said? 'Hello, Anna, I'm feeling a little suicidal today. What's new with you?'"

"You could have talked to me about it."

"Oh, I know," she said with a heavy sigh. "To tell you the truth, I was doing fine until a month or so ago. Lately, though, I've developed a major case of homesickness."

"The baby?"

"Yes. Every emotion I have lately seems directly related to the baby." She softly rubbed her stomach and shook her head. "I want to be near my family. I want to live in America. I don't think I'll ever be truly happy here. And I certainly don't want my child raised here."

"What does Marcos say?"

"My father's offered him a job with his company. He's thinking it over."

"Does Esteban know?"

"Yes. He's disappointed, but he understands. Besides, Esteban might not be here much longer himself."

"Why not?"

"He owes the government so much money in back taxes that he'll probably lose the property in the next few months."

"Lose the ranch? That's terrible! Can't he get the money from somewhere?"

"The banks won't loan it to him. He's tried."

"What about your father?"

She shook her head. "He won't help. He wants Marcos, me and the baby nearer him and Mom. He thinks we'd all be better off if the ranch were sold. It's quite a drain on everyone."

"How does Esteban feel about that?"

Hayley lifted her shoulders in a shrug. "I've never heard him speak of it, but I know this place means a lot more to him than it does to Marcos."

"Of course it does. He..."

Hayley lifted her hand. "Anna, can we please talk about something else? I want to hear more about this almost-fiancé of yours. Did you say his name was Bill?''

"Bill Ferris," Anna said, reluctantly allowing the subject to be changed.

"How did you meet?"

"He's with the company."

Hayley studied her quietly. "Well, how perfect. Your father must be pleased."

"Yes, he is. Or rather he would be, if I'd say yes," Anna said quietly, her eyes on some bright flowers.

"So what's the problem?"

"I'm not in love with him."

"I seem to recall your saying that if you found the right man—right, meaning one who fit all of your criteria—love wouldn't matter."

"Did I really say that?" Anna asked, embarrassed.

"You did.

"Time has definitely altered my way of thinking about marriage. This isn't just a business proposition. If I marry him, I'm going to have to sleep with him."

"That's usually how it works. And don't forget about having his children."

"No. That's yet another thing we agree on. He doesn't want them and neither do I."

"Has he actually asked you to marry him?"

"Um-hmm."

"What did you tell him?"

"That I was thinking it over."

"If you don't love him, I think you should just decline. Put the man out of his misery and say no."

Anna didn't say anything for a long time. "Hayley?"

"What?"

"What if it turns out that I'm someone who isn't capable of loving a man?"

"How absurd, Anna! You're one of the most loving people I know. Why would you think that?"

"Because here I am, twenty-five years old, and I never have. That can't be normal."

"You're just selective, and there's nothing wrong with that. What about Esteban?"

Anna looked at her sharply. "What about him?"

"The two of you are obviously attracted to each other. You have been since you met at my wedding. Go ahead and tell me you wouldn't like to wake up with him next to you every morning."

"Hayley! What an outrageous thing to say."

"I refuse to apologize for telling the truth."

"He is attractive, but he's not someone I could even consider allowing myself to fall in love with."

Hayley smiled. "Anna, for all of your fancy education and business acumen, you can be remarkably naive. It's not a matter of allowing yourself to fall in love. If it's meant to happen, it's going to happen, whether you *allow* it or not. Love isn't something you can program. The only problem I see with you is letting yourself acknowledge that you're in love. God forbid if the poor man isn't up to snuff in all areas of his resumé. Particularly his business qualifications."

"Why Hayley Alvarado, I believe you've developed a mean streak since you moved here."

SILHOUETTE.

 PRESENTS

A
Real Sweetheart
of a Deal!

**PEEL BACK THIS CARD AND SEE
WHAT YOU CAN GET! THEN...**

Complete the Hand Inside →

It's easy! To play your cards right,
just match this card
with the cards inside.
Turn over for more details...

Incredible, isn't it? Deal yourself in right now and get 6 fabulous gifts ABSOLUTELY FREE.

1. 4 BRAND NEW SILHOUETTE ROMANCE™ NOVELS—FREE!
Sit back and enjoy the excitement, romance and thrills of four fantastic novels. You'll receive them as part of this winning streak!

2. A LOVELY GOLD-PLATED CHAIN—
FREE! You'll love your elegant 20k gold electro-plated chain! The necklace is finely crafted with 160 double-soldered links and it's electroplate finished in genuine 20k gold. And it's yours free as added thanks for giving our Reader Service a try!

3. AN EXCITING MYSTERY BONUS—FREE!
And still your luck holds! You'll also receive a special mystery bonus. You'll be thrilled with this surprise gift. It is useful as well as practical.

PLUS

THERE'S MORE. THE DECK IS STACKED IN YOUR FAVOR. HERE ARE THREE MORE WINNING POINTS. YOU'LL ALSO RECEIVE:

4. FREE HOME DELIVERY
Imagine how you'll enjoy having the chance to preview the romantic adventures of our Silhouette heroines in the convenience of your own home. Here's how it works. Every month we'll deliver 6 new Silhouette Romance™ novels right to your door. There's no obligation to buy, and if you decide to keep them, they'll be yours for only $2.25* each! And there's no charge for postage and handling — there are no hidden extras!

5. A MONTHLY NEWSLETTER—FREE!
It's our special *"Silhouette" Newsletter* your privileged look at upcoming books and profiles of our most popular authors.

6. MORE GIFTS FROM TIME TO TIME—FREE!
It's easy to see why you have the winning hand. In addition to all the other special deals available only to our home subscribers, when you join the Silhouette Reader Service™, you can look forward to additional free gifts throughout the year.

SO DEAL YOURSELF IN – YOU CAN'T HELP BUT WIN!

* In the future, prices and terms may change but you always have the opportunity to cancel your subscription. Sales taxes applicable in NY and Iowa.
©1990 HARLEQUIN ENTERPRISES LIMITED

Remember! To win this hand, all you have to do is place your sticker inside and DETACH AND MAIL THE CARD BELOW. You'll get four free books, a free gold-plated chain and a mystery bonus.

BUT DON'T DELAY!
MAIL US YOUR LUCKY CARD TODAY!

If card is missing write to:
Silhouette Reader Service, 901 Fuhrmann Blvd., P.O. Box 1867, Buffalo, NY 14269-1867

BUSINESS REPLY CARD

First Class Permit No. 717 **Buffalo, NY**

Postage will be paid by addressee

SILHOUETTE READER SERVICE™
901 Fuhrmann Blvd.
P.O. Box 1867
Buffalo, N.Y.
14240-9952

NO POSTAGE
NECESSARY
IF MAILED
IN THE
UNITED STATES

"That's not true. I'm not mean. I'm just a bit more frank than I used to be."

"Oh, is that what you call it?"

A lovely middle-aged Spanish woman came into the courtyard. Her long hair was braided around her head and had just started to go gray. She smiled a shy greeting at Anna and bobbed her head, then spoke to Hayley in a halting combination of English and Spanish. Hayley started to say something to her, but suddenly stopped and looked at Anna. "Why am I struggling through this with you here? You can be my translator."

"I'd be happy to."

"Marcos has tried to teach me, but I'm a slow learner, and frankly I'm not really all that interested. English is difficult enough some days."

"What do you want me to say?"

"Tell her that there will be seven of us for dinner this evening."

Anna smiled at the woman. "Hello," she said in Spanish. "I'm Mrs. Alvarado's cousin Anna. And you are?"

"Carmina."

"Carmina," Anna repeated. "That's a beautiful name. Mrs. Alvarado wants me to tell you that there will be seven for dinner tonight."

Carmina inclined her head. She had the most beautiful hazel eyes.

"Anything else?" Anna asked Hayley.

"Tell her that I want the same menu we discussed earlier, with dinner to be served at 10:30."

"I understand," Carmina said without Anna translating. "Excuse me, please."

Anna watched her leave the courtyard. "With your finances being as strapped as you say they are, I'm surprised that you have a cook."

"Esteban hired her more than ten years ago. If it weren't for what she earns here, she'd have no income, at all. He even built a small home for her not far from here."

"What about her husband?"

"She's never married."

"But she's so lovely."

"I know. It's hard to understand." She tried unsuccessfully to find a comfortable sitting position.

"Can I get you a pillow or something?"

"No." She rose awkwardly to her feet. "If you don't mind, I think I'm going to lie down. I've been so tired lately. No matter how much sleep I get, it's never enough."

"I've heard that being pregnant will do that to a woman."

Hayley leaned over and kissed Anna's cheek. "Thank you for coming. I'll try to be in a better humor."

"Don't worry about your humor. I'm not going to pack and leave, just because you're in a bad mood."

Hayley smiled. "I know, but I'll try anyway. See you later, Anna. Make yourself at home."

Anna stayed in the courtyard for another hour, enjoying the coolness of the shade despite the heat of the day.

A gentle hand came down on her shoulder. She looked up and into Esteban's eyes. "Hello," she said with a warm smile.

He sat in the chair Hayley had just vacated. "That was nice," he said quietly.

"What was?"

"Coming home and having you here."

Anna's eyes met his—but then she had to look away. "I like it here. I've never been anyplace that was so utterly silent for so long."

"And you like the silence?"

"Yes."

"I do, too."

"I had a long talk with Hayley."

"That sounds very much as though you want me to ask what you talked about."

"You read me too well," she said with a smile.

"That remains to be seen."

Anna turned her head and met his gaze, to check his reaction to her words. "She's worried that you might lose the ranch."

Esteban leaned his head against the back of his chair and sighed. "That always seems to be a possibility that looms over us like an ax. I've gotten used to it."

"I know you love it here, but from what Hayley said, selling it makes a lot of sense. Then you wouldn't have to worry about the taxes any more."

"No. That's not a possibility."

"I understand that it's been in your family for a long time, but . . ."

"It's not that, Anna. There are too many people who depend on this land for their livelihoods and their homes. If the land is taken away and sold to someone else, there's no telling what would happen to them."

"That may be true, but why is it up to you to take care of all of them?"

"These people have worked this land for generations. Some of the families go back as far as the Alvarados. I can't turn my back on them now. They are my responsibility."

Anna gazed at his profile. It was impossible not to admire him. "And what happens when you run out of money?"

He was silent for a long time. "I'll find a way. I always have before."

"You could marry a wealthy woman," she teased.

He turned his head and met her gaze. "The thought has occurred to me."

There was something in the way he looked at her as he said the words that made her heart start that rhythmic beating that made her aware of its existence.

Esteban looked away. "I rejected it."

Carmina entered the courtyard carrying a tray holding a pitcher of iced orange juice and two glasses. Esteban rose and took it from her. "Thank you, Carmina."

She smiled at the two of them and left.

While Esteban set the tray on a table and poured them each a glass of juice, Anna searched her mind for an impersonal subject to discuss. "Hayley told me that you built Carmina a home here on the ranch."

"That's right."

"What happened to her family?"

"They live on the ranch."

"And they won't help her?"

"Not only won't they help her, they won't have anything to do with her."

"Why not?"

"Carmina is considered to be a fallen woman. Her family washed their hands of her years ago."

"A fallen woman? What horrible crime did she commit? Did she sleep with a man?"

"No." Esteban handed her a frosty glass. "It's a long, long story."

"I'd like to hear it if you have the time."

He sat down and leaned back in his chair. Just as Anna was thinking he wasn't going to tell her, Esteban spoke. "Life here can be harsh. There's very little money. Sometimes even food is hard to come by. As a result, parents are eager to marry off their daughters. That way they either lose that extra mouth to feed or the son-in-law moves in and provides another working body to bring home income. If a man asks to become engaged to a woman the parents almost always approve, and it doesn't matter what the girl wants. She's expected to abide by her family's wishes."

"That's horrible!"

Esteban shrugged. "It's easy to judge others when you've never suffered hardship yourself. Whether it's horrible, as you say, or not, that's the way it is and the way it's been for centuries. Engagements sometimes last for years before a marriage actually takes place. Nothing ever happens between the couple because they are always chaperoned, but if the man for some reason—and it doesn't matter how frivolous the reason is—breaks the engagement, the girl is considered to be tainted. Used. Seldom will another man ask for her hand. And the man who is her fiancé, even though he doesn't wish to have her himself, and even though he may marry someone else, will frequently treat her as his possession, so no one else would dare ask to marry her even if he wished to."

"Is that what happened to Carmina?"

"Yes and no. She was engaged, and her fiancé did decide against marrying her. But after a time he came back and asked for her hand in marriage again."

"Then everything was all right."

"Not quite. She rejected him."

"Good for her!"

"Maybe yes and maybe no. She was kicked out by her family and left to fend for herself."

"So she came here."

"She had nowhere else to go. And as it turns out, Carmina more than pays her way. I couldn't run this house without her."

"You're a good man," Anna said quietly.

Esteban turned his head and looked into her eyes.

"Excuse me," Carmina said in Spanish as she stepped into the courtyard. "There's a man here to see you, Doctor."

He looked at Anna for a moment longer, then rose and followed Carmina into the house.

Anna stared at the glass of orange juice she was holding, without really seeing it. She felt like crying and didn't know why.

Chapter Six

Anna went back to her room to finish her unpacking and dress for dinner, only to find out that someone, probably Carmina, had already done it for her.

Going through her closet, she rejected outfit after outfit as being too business-oriented. The evening clothes she'd brought were far too formal. That left her with an olive-green gathered-cotton skirt with a white sleeveless blouse and a wide rust-colored belt that emphasized her slender waist.

She'd just finished dressing when there was a knock on her door. Anna opened it to find Carmina standing there with a pair of sandals in her hand.

"The doctor told me about your poor feet," she said in Spanish. "I thought perhaps you could use these until your blisters are better."

"Thank you," Anna said with a grateful smile. "I was just thinking about how ridiculous I was going to look going downstairs barefoot for dinner with guests. Please," she said to Carmina as she stepped away from the door, "come in and keep me company while I finish getting ready."

Carmina smiled shyly back at her and stepped into the bedroom. Instead of sitting down while Anna finished brushing her hair, she hung the clothes that Anna had just taken off and reorganized the closet.

"You have such beautiful things," she said quietly as she fingered a silk dress.

"Thank you. I thought they were, too, until I got here and realized there was almost nothing I could wear on a ranch." She sat on the edge of the bed and fastened on the sandals. "Oh, these are wonderful. They don't hurt at all. Thank you."

Carmina was still standing in front of the closet.

Anna watched her. "Is there a dress that you particularly like?"

Carmina touched an emerald-green off-the-shoulder silk evening gown.

Anna joined her in front of the closet, took the dress from the rack and handed it to her. "I'd like you to have it."

Carmina put her hands behind her back and stepped away from Anna. "Oh, no, I couldn't. But thank you."

"Please. It would look beautiful on you, with your dark coloring."

Carmina shook her head.

Anna put the dress back, but decided that when she left Andalusia she'd leave the dress behind for Carmina.

Returning to the mirror, Anna studied her reflection. Her face already had enough color. Her eyes were bright and clear. Adding just a touch of lipstick, she turned to Carmina. "What do you think? Did I forget anything?"

"I think you look beautiful." Carmina stepped into the hallway and listened. "It sounds as though the guests are here. Have a good evening." With a smile at Anna, she disappeared down the other end of the hall.

Marcos and Hayley were in the foyer greeting the guests, as Anna descended the staircase. Marcos met her halfway and hugged her. "I'm glad you could come, Anna. It means a lot to us. Come meet our neighbors," he said as he took her hand and led her the rest of the way down. "This is Eduardo and Francesca Catania and their daughter Margarita."

Anna greeted them politely in Spanish as she shook their hands. The Catanias were a handsome family. The father, his dark hair just going gray at the sides, was probably in his late forties as was his wife. Their daughter was perhaps a little younger than Anna, with beautiful dark eyes and thick black hair. She was a tiny woman with very fair skin.

"Esteban is on a call, but he should be back soon," Marcos explained. "Let's sit outside and enjoy the evening." The six of them walked through the house and out another set of doors to a small but lovely garden that Anna hadn't seen before. The sun had already set, but the moon illuminated their little world.

Anna sat down on a swing seat and breathed deeply of the perfumed air. Margarita sat next to her and the two of them gently moved back and forth.

"What may I get you to drink, Anna?" Marcos asked.

"Red wine, if you have it."

He asked what the others wanted and then disappeared into the house.

Eduardo hadn't taken his eyes off Anna since they'd met and she was growing distinctly uncomfortable under his scrutiny. At first she tried to ignore him, but when that didn't work she stared back. He had the grace to look away.

Margarita touched her arm. "Please don't mind my father, Miss Bennett," she said quietly. "He's trying to assess how much of a threat you are."

"A threat?"

"To my marriage to Esteban."

Anna looked at her in surprised silence. "You're going to marry Esteban?" she finally asked.

"My father certainly thinks so. To him it's only a matter of time until Esteban proposes. He dangles his money in front of him like a carrot in front of a starving rabbit."

Margarita must be the rich woman Esteban had considered marrying. "And what do you think?" Anna asked quietly.

"I think that there was a time when Esteban wouldn't have minded an arranged marriage, but," she said looking at Anna, "that time has passed. I know it, even if my father doesn't."

"Do you love him?"

"I ask you, Miss Bennett, how could a woman not love a man like that?"

Anna raised her eyes to find Esteban walking toward them. Indeed, she thought, how could a woman not?

He greeted the Catanias with the warm friendliness of long-standing neighbors, then pulled a chair into the circle they'd formed and sank tiredly into it.

Marcos came out with a tray of drinks. "Can I get you something, Esteban?"

"No. I can't stay."

Something was wrong. Anna could see it in his expression. He answered questions and made the occasional comment, but he was obviously someplace else in his thoughts. And they weren't happy thoughts.

Esteban, as though sensing her scrutiny, looked straight at Anna. Their eyes locked. She was shocked by the depth of sadness she saw.

Taking his eyes from Anna's, he looked at his watch and rose. "If you'll excuse me, I can't stay for dinner."

As he walked from the garden into the house, Anna rose also. "I'll be right back," she said as she followed him inside and through the house to the front foyer. "Esteban?"

He turned.

"Where are you going?"

"I have a patient who's dying. There's nothing I can do about it, but I should be there."

"Who is it?"

"A child."

"I'm so sorry," she said softly.

Esteban turned his head away from her. "Please don't look at me like that, Anna. I'm hanging on to my composure by a thread, as it is."

"I'll go with you."

"No. I don't want Maximo's parents to feel they have to play host while their child lies dying."

"I understand that. I wouldn't want them to, either. I won't come in."

"I might be there all night."

"I'll wait in the truck."

Esteban looked at her for a long moment, then inclined his dark head.

"Just let me make my excuses and I'll meet you outside." She ran back through the house and would have gone into the garden but was intercepted by Marcos carrying a tray of drinks.

"Is everything all right?" he asked.

"No."

"Maximo?"

Anna nodded.

"Damn." He shook his head and his eyes filled with tears. "Even when you expect it, it's hard."

"What's wrong with him?"

"Leukemia."

"Shouldn't he be in a hospital?"

"He's been in hospitals for years. His parents brought him home to die."

Anna's throat tightened with emotion. "I'm going to go with Esteban."

"Good. I'm glad he'll have someone with him. I'll make your excuses to the others."

Anna ran back through the foyer and out the front door. Esteban was sitting in the truck with the engine running. As soon as Anna was in, he put it in gear and headed down the drive.

They traveled in silence for more than forty minutes. Anna knew instinctively that the last thing Esteban wanted to do was talk to her or anyone else.

They turned from one unlit dirt road onto another one, and followed it for a few miles. He parked in front of a tiny whitewashed house. Light shone into the yard from the open windows. After shutting off the engine, Esteban removed the keys and sat there holding them in his hand. "I think you should go back home," he said quietly.

"I'd rather wait here."

He shook his head. "I don't like the thought of you sitting out here alone."

Anna touched his arm. "Esteban, I don't want you to think about me at all right now. I'm going to stay here, and I'll be here when you come out."

He turned her hand over, placed the keys in her palm and folded her fingers closed over them. For a long time he just sat there looking at her hand, as though gathering strength for what was ahead. Without saying anything, he put Anna's hand in her lap and stepped out of the truck.

Anna's gaze followed him across the yard and into the house. Settling into her seat, she kept her eyes on the door through which he'd disappeared, trying not to think about what Maximo's family and Esteban were going through, but unable to help herself.

Hours passed, but Anna hardly noticed. Her gaze never wavered. And then he was there, standing in the doorway. A young woman and man, their arms around each other's waists, stood with him talking quietly. The woman reached up to kiss him on the cheek. The man shook his hand. A few more words were exchanged and then Esteban walked to the truck and climbed inside. He didn't look at Anna. He didn't speak. Respecting his wish for silence, Anna handed him the keys and sat quietly watching his profile as he started the engine, turned the truck around and sped down the narrow driveway. The truck picked up speed, flying through the darkness down the straightaways and careening around curves. Anna grasped the edge of her seat so hard her knuckles turned white.

The minutes ticked by. Esteban suddenly slammed on the brakes and sent the truck skidding across the loose rocks on the dirt road. Before it had even come to a complete stop, he jumped out, leaving the door gaping open behind him.

Anna watched him from the truck as the moonlight picked him out of the shadows. He stopped about fifty feet away and stood statue-still.

Anna climbed out of the truck and walked to him. For a long time she just stood there, looking at the back of his head. Reaching out a gentle hand, she touched his shoulder, but he shook her hand off and moved away from her.

Anna wasn't about to give up. He needed someone. He needed her. Standing in front of him, her gaze searched his face, trying to see what he was feeling; trying to understand what she could do to help him.

Esteban dragged his fingers through his hair and finally, for the first time since leaving Maximo's house, looked at Anna. There was such raw anguish in his face that it brought tears to her eyes. Moving her body close to his, she wrapped her arms around him.

Esteban just stood there for a moment, but then his arms wrapped around her, too, pulling her as close to him as he could. He buried his face in her neck and she could feel his tears against her skin, hot and wet. The hold he had on her was one of desperation and it threatened to crack her ribs, but she didn't care. She couldn't take his pain away, but she could share it.

When his grip relaxed a little, Anna leaned back in his arms and took his face between her hands. She kissed his cheek and then looked into his eyes. She kissed his other cheek and then looked into his eyes again. She kissed the small crease in his chin and the corners of his mouth.

Esteban suddenly cupped the back of her head in his hands and pulled her mouth to his, kissing her roughly, jerking her body back against his. He wasn't crying any longer. He was angry. It was evident in every taut muscle of his body, in his ragged breathing, even in the way he was holding Anna.

They went down on their knees. Esteban pulled her blouse out from her skirt and tried to unbutton it, but the buttons were small and he didn't have the patience to bother with them at the moment. Instead he put his hand between their two bodies, grasped her blouse at the top and ripped it down to her waist.

The sound brought him back to his senses. He leaned back, away from her, his breathing harsh, and looked at what he'd done. "Oh, God, Anna," he said softly, as he tried to pull the two ends of her blouse together. "I'm so sorry."

She put her hands over his and held them between her breasts. "It's all right. I understand. You need to feel close to someone right now and I'm here." Letting her own blouse fall open, Anna unbuttoned his shirt and slid it from his shoulders, then moved back into his arms and pressed her body against his.

Esteban rubbed his cheek against her silky hair. The arms holding Anna this time had a gentle strength. "I'm glad you're with me," he said quietly.

Anna leaned back and looked into his eyes.

Esteban trailed the backs of his fingers over the smooth skin of her cheek, his eyes following their movement. "How is it that I, who never needed anyone before, now find that I need you very much?" His eyes moved to hers. "And what am I going to do about that need when you're gone?"

"It's not me," she said softly. "It's the circumstances. It's tonight, not tomorrow."

"Ahh." Esteban put his finger under her chin and gazed at her lovely face. Ever so slowly, he lowered his mouth to hers.

Anna's lips parted softly. Gently, as though in slow motion, they explored each other. A vivid warmth grew deep inside her and spread.

Esteban lowered her to the ground. Rolling up his shirt, he pillowed her head on it, then with his body half covering hers, their bare skin touching, he kissed her again. Raising himself over her, he gazed into her eyes as he pushed her hair away from her face. He kissed the corners of her mouth, then moved his body lower on hers. With a sigh that seemed to come from his soul, he wrapped his arms around her waist, rested his head between her throat and the swell of her breasts and lay still.

Anna smoothed his hair with a tender touch and placed her lips against his head.

The night passed like that, with the two of them awake but unmoving. Anna stared at the stars, aware of the man lying against her, holding on to her. And she, who'd never slept outside in her life, nor been with a man, felt as though she were right where she should have been. It was this place and this man.

When the sun started to rise, Esteban stirred. Wordlessly he raised himself over Anna and looked into her eyes. With exquisite gentleness, he lingeringly kissed her warm, full lips. Then getting to his feet, he helped Anna up, shook the leaves from the shirt that had pillowed her head and slipped it protectively over her arms and shoulders.

Anna's eyes watched his face as he buttoned it for her. When he'd finished, Esteban met her gaze. As though he couldn't help himself, he pulled her into his arms and held her.

Then with a sigh he kissed her forehead, turned and led her to the truck. As soon as she was settled inside, he closed the door, walked around to the driver's side and started the engine.

No words passed between them on the drive home. When they arrived, he parked in front. The sun was almost completely up. Anna climbed out and closed the door. She stood there with her hands on the door, looking at Esteban through the open window. Then she slowly turned and started to go into the house.

"Anna?"

She looked back at him.

"Thank you."

Anna inclined her head and went into the house.

Esteban stayed where he was, deep in thought, his hands on the steering wheel.

When Anna got to her room, she leaned her back against the door and stood there absolutely still. Her chest was tight with an emotion she didn't understand. An emotion that she knew instinctively she'd be better off ignoring.

She took a deep breath and slowly exhaled, then took another one and did the same. For the first time since walking into her room, she focused and found her bed turned down and a nightgown laid out. Taking off Esteban's shirt she started to lay it down, but instead she slowly raised it to her face, rubbing the material against her cheek and breathing in his scent. As soon as she realized what she was doing, she shook her head and tossed it carelessly over the back of a chair.

The shutters in her windows were closed to keep out the heat of the day, making the room comfortably dim despite the early morning sunlight. Anna left the nightgown where it was and lay on her bed. Very gradually her eyes began to close. She was so tired. Not just physically this time, but emotionally.

At last sleep drifted over her like a welcome blanket, shutting off the thoughts she didn't dare let herself have.

"Anna? Anna, wake up."

Anna opened her eyes and found herself looking at Hayley as her cousin bent over her. "Is something wrong?" She rose up on her elbows. "Are you all right?"

"I'm fine." Her eyes went to Anna's ripped blouse and widened. "What happened to you?"

Anna pulled the edges of her blouse together as she sat up. "An accident. Nothing important. What time is it?"

"Seven-thirty."

Anna sank back against her pillows. "Hayley, I just got home a little while ago. What do you want?"

"You had a phone call last night."

"My dad?"

"Bill Ferris."

"Oh."

"He wanted you to call him back, and when you didn't he called again. Actually he called four times, in all."

"I'm sorry."

"That's all right. I wasn't complaining. I just didn't know what to tell him."

"What's wrong with the truth?"

"That you were with Esteban all night? I didn't think he would have taken it very well."

"I hadn't thought about that," Anna said with a sigh. "I'll call him back this afternoon."

Hayley was sitting on the edge of the bed. "So were you?" she asked.

"Was I what?"

Hayley looked from her blouse to Esteban's shirt. "With Esteban?"

"Yes, but not in the way you're thinking."

"Why not?"

"Hayley!"

"He's attracted to you; you're attracted to him. You were with him all night. Why didn't anything happen?"

"You've really changed since you came to Spain," Anna said as she left the bed and went into her closet. "A year ago you would never have asked me a question like that."

"Probably not," she said without remorse. "So why didn't anything happen between you and Esteban?"

Anna looked at her in exasperation. "I have no intention of answering."

"Well, it was worth a shot."

Anna pulled a full blue skirt out and held it against herself. "Do you have a blouse that would go with this? I brought a matching sweater, but it's too heavy for this weather."

"I think I can find something."

"Thanks. I'm going to take a shower and change, then I'll come downstairs and we can do something together."

"Is that your polite way of telling me that you don't want to talk about this anymore?"

Anna smiled at her. "Not very subtle, am I?"

"No, but then neither am I." Hayley struggled to her feet. "I'll bring the blouse right away."

As soon as the door closed behind her cousin, Anna slipped out of her clothes and into a light robe that she belted at her waist. Crossing to the window, she pushed open the shutters. Bright sunlight streamed in.

She heard the horse before she saw it, its hooves thudding softly in the grass. Leaning further out her window, she saw it round a corner with Esteban on its back.

As though sensing that she was there, Esteban stopped immediately beneath her window and looked up. Their eyes met and held.

The huge horse reared suddenly, but Esteban remained at ease as he brought its front hooves back to the ground, his eyes never leaving Anna's. With a slight inclination of his head, he wheeled the horse around and rode away, around the corner of the house and out of her line of vision.

She jumped at the sharp sound of a knock on the door. "Come in."

Carmina opened the door. "Excuse me. There is a telephone call for you."

"Thank you. Where's the nearest phone?"

"The only one is in the doctor's library. I'll show you where it is."

Anna tightened the belt of her robe as they went down the stairs and into Esteban's small but well-stocked library. As she went to the desk, Carmina left the room, closing the doors after her. Anna lifted the receiver to her ear, knowing before she spoke who was at the other end.

"Anna!" Bill Ferris said. "I've been trying to contact you since last night your time."

"I know."

"Where were you? I was worried."

"I'm fine. I was going to call you later. Was there something specific you needed to talk to me about?"

"Frankly, I wanted to know how your cousin is doing."

"She's fine."

"Any idea when you'll be coming back to work?"

"I'd planned on staying here for at least one week. Perhaps even two."

"That long?"

She found his tone annoying. "We've already been through all this, Bill."

"I know, but you should see the way your backlog is building up. Your father's finding the whole situation quite exasperating and inconvenient."

"If my father is exasperated and inconvenienced, as you say, he's perfectly capable of telling me that himself."

There was a long pause. "Anna, is something wrong? You sound strange."

"I just don't like it when you take it upon yourself to run interference between my father and me. We somehow managed to communicate our feelings to each other just fine before you came to work for Bennett Industries, Bill."

"I'm sorry."

Anna closed her eyes and shook her head. "Oh, I'm the one who should apologize. That was a rotten thing to say. I guess I'm a little tired."

"It's all right. I understand. Besides, I wasn't really calling about business. That was just an excuse. What I was really calling about was to ask if you'd given any more thought to my proposal."

"Yes," she said quietly, "I have."

"And?"

"I'm sorry, Bill, but I can't marry you." She hadn't even realized that she'd made a decision until the words were spoken. But as soon as they were, she felt the most blessed sense of relief. This chapter was over.

"Look," he said, backtracking, "I'm pushing you. Maybe you need to think about it a little longer."

"No. I've made up my mind."

"It would work between us, Anna."

"No, it wouldn't."

"But we talked about this before you went to Spain. You weren't nearly so sure then."

"I am now."

"Why?"

"I don't know, Bill. It's not something I can explain. It just is."

"Your father's going to be very disappointed."

She tried to hold on to her temper. "Once again, that's between my father and me."

"Anna, I—"

"I don't want to talk about this any more. I'm sorry if you're disappointed, but I'm not going to change my mind."

There was a long pause. "All right. I won't mention it again. Everything will be business as usual."

"Thank you."

"Goodbye, Anna."

"Goodbye."

After she'd hung up Anna sat in Esteban's chair staring out the window, her hand on her stomach.

"Hello, Anna."

Startled, she turned in the chair to find Esteban standing in the doorway. "I thought you'd be sleeping."

"Hayley couldn't restrain her curiosity." She looked at his shadowed, unshaven face. "Are you all right, Esteban?" she asked softly.

He sat in a chair across from her. "Better than I was last night. Thank you for sticking it out with me."

Her eyes met his.

"Anna, what's wrong?"

She shook her head, not trusting her voice. She didn't even know what was wrong.

"Did you just get some bad news on the phone?"

She cleared her throat. "No. I had to deliver some, though. It was more difficult than I expected it to be."

"Do you want to talk about it?"

"No. Thank you, anyway."

His tawny gaze moved over her face.

Anna got quickly to her feet—too quickly. She had to grip the edge of the desk to keep her balance.

Esteban was instantly beside her, his hands at her waist to give her support.

She smiled reassuringly at him. "Sorry. I got up a little too fast."

"Are you sure that's all it is?"

"I'm sure." She moved away from him.

"When was the last time you had a real meal?"

"On the plane, I guess."

"Have you had anything since the orange yesterday morning?"

She thought for a moment. "No."

"Oh, Anna Bennett, you must take better care of yourself," he said as he put his arm around her. "Come on. I'll cook you something."

"That's not necessary. I can do it myself."

"You can hardly stand up."

Anna stood firm as she looked up at him. "Esteban, you have a lot more important things to do than take care of me." She touched his beard-shadowed cheek with gentle fingertips. "Look at you. You haven't even had a chance to shave yet."

He covered her hand with his and held it against his face. "I don't know if this makes any sense to you, Anna, but right now I need to take care of you. Let me."

She gave her silent consent and the two of them went downstairs to the kitchen. It was old-fashioned and immaculate. Esteban seated her at a small, round table in the center of the room and went straight to the refrigerator.

"I know it's a little early for lunch, but I make a terrific sandwich."

"That's fine."

He loaded his arms with ingredients and carried everything to the counter. Anna had to admit that she enjoyed watching him. It was obvious that he was no stranger to the kitchen. And the ham sandwiches he put together were nothing less than works of art. "I'm really surprised," she said as he sat across from her.

"About what?"

She indicated the sandwiches with a wave of her hand. "That you could do this."

"I'm a very domestic man," he said with a smile, as he looked into her eyes.

"I'm afraid I'm not domestic, at all." Anna took a bite of her sandwich and sighed. "This is wonderful," she said as she swallowed. "Ten minutes ago I didn't feel hungry, at all, and now I could eat forever."

He took a bite of his own sandwich. "Have you ever had a chance to be domestic?"

"Let's see," she said thoughtfully. "I used to make popcorn when I visited Hayley's house."

Esteban smiled. "Other than that?"

"Not really. I've always had maids to cook for me and clean up after me."

"You've led a very pampered life."

She took another bite of her sandwich. "Since coming here, I'm almost ashamed of it. I've never felt that way before."

"And you shouldn't feel that way now. People do the best they can with what they have. You happen to have had a bit more than most."

"I'm surprised you don't hold it against me."

"Why would I do that?"

"Some people do."

"I'm not some people."

"I've noticed that."

"And what else have you noticed, Anna Bennett?"

Her gaze locked with his. "That you have the most wonderful eyes I've ever seen."

The grooves in his cheeks deepened, embarrassing her.

"Don't laugh at me."

"I'm not laughing at you, Anna. I think you're completely charming."

She was strangely disconcerted by his directness and lowered her eyes.

"What are you thinking?"

She shook her head. "I've been trying not to think since I got here."

"Why?"

"It seems to be easier that way."

"So you're planning on sort of drifting through your time in Andalusia and waiting until you get back to your own world to truly exist."

"Something like that."

"What are you afraid of?"

She looked up sharply. "I'm not afraid."

"Yes you are. And when you let yourself think about it, not only will you realize that it's true, you'll also understand the reason behind your fear."

"You sound as though you already know."

He took another bite of his sandwich. "I do."

"Then why don't you explain it to me?"

He shook his head. "This is something you must come to understand on your own."

Marcos walked into the kitchen to talk to Esteban, leaving Anna to ponder his words. Was she truly afraid? And if she was, of what?

Chapter Seven

Anna left the hacienda and headed out across the grounds, walking in a different direction from any she'd taken on the other walks. She'd been in Spain for nearly a week and was growing used to the slower pace. What amazed her more than anything else was that she wasn't at all bored. Things here were exactly as they should be. Quiet, but no less interesting.

"Anna!"

She stopped walking and turned to find Esteban walking toward her from the stables.

"Where are you going?" he asked as he drew even with her. "Anywhere in particular?"

"Just for a walk."

"You've been doing a lot of walking lately. I would have thought you'd have had more than enough after your first day in the country."

"Now that my feet don't hurt any more, I've discovered that I actually enjoy walking."

"If that's the case, how would you like to see the old hacienda of my ancestors?"

"I'd love it. Do you have time to take me?"

"Not really, but I need the break." They fell into step together. "It's not too far from here."

"I think I'd like you to give me that in miles. I don't trust your version of what's too far and what isn't," she said with a smile.

"Two miles."

"I can handle that."

"I haven't seen much of you lately. What have you been doing with your time?" he asked.

"Keeping Hayley company, for the most part. That's why I'm here, after all. But when she's sleeping, or just not in the mood for company, I wander around."

"Now that you've been here for a while, what do you think of my Andalusia?"

"I love it," she said quietly. "It's not like any place I've ever been before. I wish I could get Hayley to see it through my eyes."

"That would be nice, Anna, but I'm afraid it's not going to happen."

"What will you do if they leave?"

"You mean *when* they leave." He shook his head. "I don't know, yet. I'm sure I can get help from some of the men who live on the ranch."

Anna glanced sideways at him. "I've been thinking about your tax problem."

"Why?"

"Because I can help you."

"I don't need your help."

"Yes, you do. I have the money and you don't. I've got nothing I need to spend it on, and you do."

"I'm not a charity case." He wasn't angry, but there was iron in his voice.

"No, you're not. But you've got something very worthwhile here. You're needed and your land is needed."

"I'm well aware of that, Anna. And I'll find a way to keep things as they are."

"Without my help?"

"Without it."

"I could loan it to you. You could pay me back as soon as you're able."

Esteban stopped walking and turned to face Anna. "You've got a good heart and I know you mean well, Anna, but you are the last person in the world I would ever take money from."

She looked into his eyes. "Why? I have it, and you need it. A perfect combination."

A corner of his mouth lifted. "Stop arguing with me and just accept my decision. I won't change my mind."

Anna sighed. "I had a feeling you were going to be difficult about it. Do you have something specific that you can do to raise the money?"

"Yes."

"What?"

"You're much too nosy for your own good," he said as he started walking again.

Anna fell into step beside him. "I prefer to think of myself as curious."

"I'm sure you do."

"So what are you going to do?"

Esteban shook his head and smiled. "Nosy *and* persistent. It's none of your business."

"If I weren't being so rude myself, I'd tell you how rude you're being."

He touched her arm and pointed at something in the distance. It looked like the ruins of a small town. As they got closer, Anna could see the Moorish lines of what once must have been a magnificent home. They cut across a large field and headed up a hill that was filled with the rubble of the home. Anna stepped over the stones bleached white by the merciless sun and over low walls, some almost entirely covered by a fine dirt that was more like sand that had been blown over the centuries.

There were still some tiles intact, though not many, and no complete walls. She could see where there had been an indoor pool of some sort.

Esteban watched Anna as she moved through the ruins, touching this and that, and found himself wondering what his Moorish ancestors would have thought of such an angelic-looking creature, with her bright gold hair, wandering through their home. She was wearing another one of Hayley's skirts, full and brightly colored. It floated gracefully around her slender figure. She turned and smiled at him, and Esteban's heart caught.

"This is wonderful," she said softly.

"Why are you whispering?"

"A place like this demands it, don't you think?" she asked as she sat on one of the low walls and gazed out at the rest of the world.

He sat next to her. "You're right," he said after a while.

"Do you ever come here just to sit?"

"Sometimes."

"I think I'd do that a lot if I lived here."

"Like your rock."

Anna smiled, her gaze still on the vista. "Like my rock. I guess I just enjoy having special places. Have you ever been here at night when there's a full moon?"

"Yes."

"I bet there's an almost mystical feeling, with ghostly spirits of the people who once lived here." Her voice was still a whisper as she looked at him. "What do you think?"

"I think you have a vivid imagination."

"You seem surprised."

"I guess I thought you'd be more of the I'll-believe-it-when-I-see-it-school of philosophy."

"Intrepid traveler and metaphysical thinker. I wonder what I'll surprise you with next?"

"Do you enjoy surprising people?"

"I enjoy surprising you."

"Why?"

"Because I think you like to pigeonhole people, and you can't always do that."

"So I'm learning. And what are you learning, Anna?"

A smile touched her mouth. "Not to pigeonhole myself. There's a whole world beyond mine that I never knew existed. And even if I had known it existed, I wouldn't have been interested in discovering it."

"But in this instance your hand was forced."

"You could say that. I'd do anything for Hayley, and she knows it."

"Including coming here."

There was a smile behind Anna's eyes as she glanced at him. "Believe me, at the time I thought it was quite a sacrifice. I had visions of myself becoming eligible for sainthood in a few hundred years."

Esteban laughed. "I can imagine."

"But now that I'm here, I'm glad of it."

His eyes moved over her profile. "So am I."

Anna sensed the look and turned her head. Her eyes locked with his. She could feel the movement of her pulse at the base of her throat. It was all she could do to force her eyes away from his. "What time is it?" she asked, as though it mattered.

Esteban looked at his watch. "Just after five."

"I didn't realize that it was so late. I have to be getting back. Hayley will be wondering where I am."

Esteban rose and held out his hand. "Come on. I'll go back with you."

She let him help her to her feet, but quickly retrieved her hand. They walked together quite companionably. It surprised Anna that she could feel so comfortable with someone who also made her very much aware that she was a woman.

When they arrived at the house, there were some people waiting for them. Esteban went straight to a woman who was holding a baby. He smiled as he took

the child from her and asked her some questions.
There were also two men, one of whom was holding
his arm as though it was injured, another woman and
several other children.

Esteban handed the child back to its mother and
went to the obviously injured man. "Anna," he said
without looking at her, "will you help me, please?"

"Help you what?"

"With these people."

"Of course." She followed him to the tiny building
he used as a clinic, set not far from the house. Inside
were two rooms. One was a waiting area, with a desk
and some cheap plastic chairs; the other was where he
saw his patients.

"There's an index card in the box on the desk for
everyone who's here. Find each one and send them in
with the patients, as I see them."

"All right," she said as she settled herself into the
chair behind the desk. "Anything else?"

"Not unless you have some nurse's training that you
haven't told me about."

"I'm afraid not."

"That's all, then. And Anna?"

She looked up. "Yes?"

"Thank you."

"You're welcome," she said with a smile.

As soon as he'd disappeared into the other room,
Anna looked at the people sitting with her. She introduced herself, then began asking who they were and
finding the appropriate cards.

In about twenty minutes, Esteban came out with the
man, whose arm was now in a cast. He gave him some

instructions and sent him on his way. Next were the mother and baby. He took the child again and carried him into the other room. All that was needed was a booster shot, but everybody winced when the baby cried.

With the child sniffing and whimpering and held tightly in its mother's arms, Esteban leaned over the desk and wrote some instructions about when she was to return for the next shot. After handing the woman a note, he rested his hand on the baby's head and spoke softly. Much to Anna's amazement, the child grew quiet.

Anna looked at Esteban's face. His caring, his compassion, were there for anyone to see.

It took about an hour to see the rest of the people who were waiting. Anna spent her time talking to them, trying to put them at ease. The adults were more nervous than the chidren, and it was a little harder to take their minds off the purpose of their visit.

As soon as the last one had left, Esteban sat on the edge of the desk and smiled at Anna. "Nice job."

"I didn't do anything."

"You made them feel comfortable. Not everyone can do that. And you stuck it out. You could have left as soon as you found the cards for everyone."

"And miss watching you in action? Never."

Esteban smiled at her. "Not very exciting, I'm afraid."

"Perhaps not. But it was enlightening."

"Enlightening?"

Anna nodded. "You're so tall and so strong that your gentleness with these people is quite a contrast."

"Is that good or bad?"

"Very good."

Esteban looked at his watch. "If you were in trouble with Hayley before, you're really going to be on her bad side now. It's after eight."

Anna got quickly to her feet. "I had no idea it was so late. She's going to think I dropped off the edge of the earth."

"Then we'd better let her know everything's all right." He turned off the lights and opened the door for her. As she walked past him, her arm brushed against his. She stopped for a moment and looked up at him. Their eyes met and held. Whenever she looked at him, it was hard to look away.

But she did, and started walking. Esteban closed up the clinic and fell into step with her. As soon as they entered the house, Hayley loomed in front of them, her hands on her hips. "Well, how nice of you to show up for dinner."

"I'm sorry," Anna said contritely. "The time just got away from me."

"You could try wearing a watch."

"It's the first time I can remember ever going an entire week without a watch."

"I think I'll let the two of you settle this," Esteban said as he moved past them and went up the stairs.

"I take it you were together?" Hayley said.

"Yes."

"And you still claim that nothing is going on? Anna, I've been around the block once or twice."

"We're..." Anna shook her head. "I don't know what we are. Friends isn't quite the word I'm looking for. I just know that I thoroughly enjoy the man's company."

"Humph."

"You're not really mad at me, are you? I wasn't late intentionally."

"Well, I suppose not," Hayley relented. "But you're supposed to be here to visit me."

"I know. I'll do better tomorrow."

"I sound like a whiny brat, don't I?" Hayley asked with a chagrined smile.

"I couldn't have described it better myself."

"Sorry."

"That's all right. How about if I tell you right away, next time, so we can nip any whining in the bud."

"That sounds good in theory, but I'll probably take your head off in practice."

"I'll risk it."

Hayley looped her arm through Anna's. "Come on. We're going to eat in the courtyard tonight."

Esteban hadn't joined them for dinner. He rarely did. Sometimes Anna felt as though he was avoiding her, and other times she felt as though he was seeking her out. It was confusing.

Hayley and Marcos went to bed early. Anna tried to but couldn't sleep. Getting out of bed, she put her flowing floor-length white cotton robe over a matching nightgown and went downstairs.

Everything was dark. No one was up. She stepped outside and breathed deeply of the night air. There was a half-moon, but it was surprisingly bright and large as it hung low in the sky.

Without really thinking about it, she lifted the hems of her robe and nightgown and headed toward the ruins.

When they first came into view, she stopped and just looked at them from a distance. In the moonlight they truly appeared haunting, and she knew that the sight of them just the way they were at that moment in the half-moon light was something she'd carry with her for the rest of her life.

Anna moved silently forward across the field and up the hill until she was in the ruins. Walking to a low wall, she stood on it and raised her face to the sky. Other women in other centuries had looked out from here and seen this very same moon.

A light breeze molded her nightgown to the front of her body and sent it billowing behind her.

The man on the horse watched her quietly from a distance, silhouetted as she stood there like some ancient goddess. An apparition. She was absolutely still.

Anna heard the horse before she saw it. When it stopped in front of her, she lowered her eyes from the moon and looked at Esteban.

"You're going to catch a cold out here, dressed like that," he said quietly.

"I don't even care."

"Well I do." He moved the horse closer to the wall, put his arm around Anna's waist and lifted her sideways onto the horse in front of him. "What are you doing here?"

"I wanted to see it at night." She looked up into his eyes. "Why are you here?"

"I couldn't sleep."

"That seems to be going around."

He raised his hand to trace the line of her jaw. "I take it you couldn't sleep, either."

"Some nights are harder than others."

"Why was tonight so difficult?"

"I couldn't shut my mind down."

"Business or personal?"

"I don't know. It's as though I'm on the verge of some major discovery or revelation that I can't quite focus on yet, and the harder I try the more it eludes me."

His gaze moved over her face. "So you came here."

"Like you." Their lips were only a whisper away from touching. "Why couldn't you sleep?"

"A lot of reasons."

"Are you on the verge of some major revelation, too?"

"No. I've had mine."

"Tell me about it."

A corner of his mouth lifted. "No."

"None of my business?"

"I'll tell you in time."

"I'll be gone in a week."

"I know." His eyes moved over her face. "I know," he repeated softly as his mouth covered hers.

Anna's fingers tangled in his thick hair, pulling him closer, but the kiss remained gentle. Esteban made sure of it. He rubbed his lips over hers; kissed the corners of her mouth and the tip of her nose.

The horse moved restlessly beneath them, stamping his hooves and shaking his head.

Esteban smiled into her eyes. "My horse appears to be restless."

Anna kissed her way along his jaw and nuzzled his ear. "He's just jealous."

"Anna..."

"Umm. You always smell so good," she whispered next to his ear.

"It's a curse."

Anna leaned back and smiled up at him in the moonlight. "What's next?"

"I take you back to the house."

"Why?"

"Because that's the way it has to be for now," he replied.

"That doesn't answer my question."

"I know."

"You do that to me a lot."

"What kind of answer do you want?" he asked.

"I guess I want to understand why, when we're so obviously attracted to each other, you won't take our relationship that one step further."

"Are you asking me, in your own inimitable way, why we haven't made love yet?"

"Yes."

"Because there are certain things that have to happen first. Making love with you isn't something I could ever take lightly. It's not a moment of passion. There's a lot more to it than that. And now, if that's the end of your interrogation," he said as he kneed his horse, "we're going home."

No one had been more surprised by her question than Anna. But then, things were happening around her—and inside her—that she didn't understand.

Chapter Eight

A week later Anna was sitting quietly in the courtyard with Hayley, reading.

Or at least she was trying to read. Her thoughts kept
wandering off. It seemed as though every time she
tried to focus on the words, all she could see was
Esteban.

She'd avoided him as much as was possible under
the circumstances. And when it wasn't possible, she
made sure she wasn't alone with him. Not because she
didn't enjoy his company—but because she did.

"What's that?" Hayley asked.

Anna looked up. "What's what?"

"That thing you're reading."

Anna sighed as she closed the cover of the ring
binder. "A prospectus on the company Dad wants to
take over."

"Sounds exciting."

"No comment."

"Was that what your father called you about this morning?"

"That and a few other things. He wants me to get back to work the day after tomorrow."

"But you've only been here for two weeks."

"I know."

"Are you going?"

"I think so. This is the most time I've taken off since I joined the company."

"And it's still standing."

"Not to hear my father tell it," she said with a smile.

"What if neither Esteban nor Marcos has the time to take you to the airport?"

"I wouldn't put myself through that trip again, anyway. A helicopter makes a lot more sense."

An agitated Carmina walked into the courtyard. "Excuse me," she said in rapid Spanish, "but I must find the doctor right away."

"What's wrong?" Anna asked.

"There's a boy here. He says his cousin is very sick and needs help."

Anna turned to Hayley. "Do you know where Esteban is?"

"He said something about fixing some fences in one of the pastures."

"Do you remember which pasture?"

"I'm not sure. I think the northernmost one, with the cattle in it. I know he took the truck."

"Where's Marcos?"

"He went into the village this morning, about a two-hour drive from here."

"So how can we get in touch with Esteban?"

"The only way is to go find him."

"But there's no car or truck."

"There are the horses," Carmina suggested.

Anna looked at Hayley, who immediately patted her stomach. "Don't even think it."

"But I can't ride a horse," Anna said in distress. She looked hopefully at Carmina. "What about you?"

Carmina took a step back. "No. I'm afraid of them. One kicked me when I was a child."

"I guess that leaves you," Hayley said quietly.

Anna's heart sank. Rising from her chair, she dropped the file she'd been reading onto Hayley's lap. "If my neck gets broken when the horse throws me, tell my father to read the notes I made in the margins. How do I get to Esteban?"

"As you leave the stables, follow the road to the right and keep going right at any forks you come to. It'll take you straight to the pasture, but once you get there you're on your own. I don't know what part of it he's working on."

"If he's there, I'll find him." She walked toward Carmina and followed her into the house. "Where's the boy?"

"Waiting in the hall."

He couldn't have been more than ten, and very small. Anna put her hands on his shoulders. "What's your name?" she asked in Spanish, her voice low and soothing.

"Pedro."

"Pedro what?"

"Dominguez."

"Well, Pedro, I'm going to go get the doctor for your cousin. Does he know where you live?"

The boy nodded rapidly.

"All right. What exactly is wrong with—is it him or her?"

"Her," the child replied. "She's been sick."

"Sick in what way?"

"She's had a bad cold. Trouble breathing. Coughing. This morning she didn't get out of bed."

"Has she been sick long?"

"A week. But not like this morning."

"Could you talk to her this morning? Was she awake?"

He nodded.

"At least she was conscious. That's good. What I need for you to do now, Pedro, is go home. I'll get the doctor there as soon as I can."

"All right." Without saying anything else, Pedro turned and ran.

Anna looked down at her long, full skirt. It was completely wrong for horseback riding, but she didn't want to take the time to change. She'd already started through the door when Hayley called out to her.

Anna turned. "I have to go."

"I know, but it suddenly occurred to me that if you don't know how to ride a horse, you certainly don't know how to saddle one."

"True."

"I can at least help with that."

The two women hurried as quickly as they could to the stables. Esteban's big horse was in one of the stalls. Hayley pointed to a saddle hanging on the wall. "Lift that down."

While Anna did that, Hayley led the horse from the stall and tethered it to the stall gate.

"Now put the saddle on Gitano's back."

Anna did.

Hayley was fairly agile, considering the size of her stomach. In just a few minutes, the horse was ready.

"Okay," Hayley said, breathing hard as she straightened. "Hop on."

"Just like that?"

"Just like that. Then we'll check the stirrups."

Anna, her heart in her throat, mounted the horse and looked nervously down at Hayley. "I feel like I'm on the top floor of the Sears Tower."

"He's a big one, isn't he? Get your skirt out of the way and bend your knees just a little."

Anna hiked up her skirt, exposing her long legs, letting the rest of it drift over the back of the horse.

Hayley adjusted first the left stirrup and then the right. "Put your feet in them and see how they feel."

Anna did. "How are they supposed to feel?"

"Comfortable."

Anna lifted an expressive brow. "You can't be serious."

"All right. As comfortable as they can feel under the circumstances."

"That's better. They feel fine—under the circumstances."

"You're all set, then."

"What do I do now?"

"Well, when you want Gitano to move, you lightly squeeze him with your knees."

"What about when I want him to stop?"

"Pull back on the reins, but not too hard. He's a good horse. He'll know what to do. And keep the reins short. That'll help you maintain control."

"All right. I guess that's it, then." She looked down at Hayley. "Hope to see you later."

Hayley smiled. "You will."

"How will I know which is the northernmost pasture, when I get there? Is there some kind of sign?"

"No." Hayley thought for a moment. "Look for a triangle of wild olive trees to the right of the road. The pasture is less than a mile from those trees."

"Olive trees. And how long of a ride is it?"

"If you ride full out, an hour. If not, longer."

"Definitely longer."

"Just do the best you can."

"That's the story of my life." Ever so carefully, she squeezed the horse with her knees. He left the stables at a slow trot with Anna bouncing in the saddle.

After a few minutes, she got used to the movement and grew less afraid of falling. She started experimenting with ways of holding herself so that she rode more with the horse's movement than against it and discovered that if she let her body relax, his rhythm became hers.

Feeling braver, she encouraged him to go a little faster—but only a little.

There were so many ways things could be improved. Esteban shouldn't have to have someone riding around trying to find him. He should have a beeper, or a cellular telephone. He should have a helicopter to enable him to get around more quickly. This was ridiculous.

When she finally spotted the olive trees, she was ready to kiss the ground they grew on. And as Hayley had said, about a mile beyond that spot she saw the pasture and left the road to follow the line of the fence. She'd done that for nearly half an hour when she spotted the truck. Esteban was about twenty yards away from the truck, his shirt off as he hammered in a new fence post, his upper body covered wtih sweat.

"Esteban!" she called out.

He looked up in surprise as she rode toward him. "What are you doing here?" he asked.

She stopped the horse in front of him and slid to the ground. "A little boy named Pedro Dominguez came to the house. He said that his cousin is sick and needs you."

"Did he say what was wrong?" Esteban asked as he grabbed a towel and wiped himself down.

"Yes. He said that she's had a cough and congestion and didn't get out of bed this morning."

"How long has she been sick?"

"About a week."

"A week?"

"Yes."

He shook his head. "No matter how many times I tell them to get me right away, they just won't do it until they absolutely have no choice."

"A lot of people are like that."

"You?"

"I'm very bad about doctors. I always figure I'll feel better if I just wait it out."

"That could be dangerous."

"I'm still here."

He glanced at her as he loaded his tools into the back of the truck. "So what do you want to do, Anna? Go with me, or ride Gitano back home?"

The thought of sitting on that horse all the way back was more than she cared to contemplate. "I'll go with you," she answered without missing a beat.

"All right." He unsaddled the horse and slapped its rump. The horse took off in the direction of home and Esteban tossed the saddle into the truck.

"Thank you," she said gratefully as she climbed into the passenger seat. "Pedro said you knew where he lived."

"I do." He put the truck into gear and roared off, leaving a trail of dust behind them.

Anna bounced back in her seat and grimaced.

"Sorry," Esteban said as he slowed a little. "How did you manage to ride a horse all that way?"

"I have no idea."

"Are you all right?"

"I didn't fall off, if that's what you mean."

He smiled and shook his head. "You constantly surprise me, Anna."

"I know the feeling. Lately I've surprised myself. It's as though someone else's mind is inhabiting my body, making it do strange and painful things."

"One day they'll combine to make the real you."

"Sometimes I wonder who the real me is," she said quietly.

"Anna Bennett, daughter of Charles Bennett, vice-president of Bennett Industries, future CEO."

She turned her head and gazed at his profile. "I'm much more than that."

"I know. I wasn't sure that you did."

Anna was quietly thoughtful as they drove.

Esteban looked at her for a moment, then turned his attention back to the road. "Have you been avoiding me lately, Anna?"

"Yes."

"Why?"

"It just seemed the easiest thing to do."

"Anna..."

"I don't want to talk about it."

"We're going to talk about it," he said as he parked the car in front of a tiny home that was little more than a shack, "but not right now."

Several very dirty children ran up to the truck—none over the age of ten. Anna counted eight of them. Esteban greeted them all by name as he climbed out and picked the smallest little girl up in his arms to give her a hug and a smile. Pedro stood in the door of the house. "Please," he called out in excited Spanish, "you must come now."

Esteban handed the little girl to Anna and walked quickly into the house. The little girl, her brown face still round with baby fat, sucked her thumb as she stared at Anna's golden hair.

Anna smiled at her. "Who are you?" she asked in Spanish.

She didn't say anything.

"That's Jenetta," one of the boys told her.

"Does she talk?"

"Not to strangers."

Jenetta struggled and Anna set her gently on the ground. As she straightened, she really looked around for the first time and was shocked by the poverty. She'd never seen anything like it. The house hadn't been kept up at all. Broken furniture, old mattresses, rusting farm implements and things she didn't recognize littered the front of the house.

Esteban came out of the house carrying a woman who looked to be no more than twenty in his arms.

"Open the passenger door, Anna."

She did. "What's wrong with her?"

"Pneumonia, for one. Her fever's very high. There are some tests I need to run on her, and I can't do it here." He placed the woman in the truck and covered her with a blanket. "I have to go into the city."

"What can I do to help?"

He looked at her apologetically. "I'm sorry, Anna, but I'm going to have to ask you to stay here with the children. There's no one else."

Anna looked at the children and then at Esteban. "But I've never been around children. I don't have the faintest idea what to do with them."

"Just make sure they get fed and keep out of trouble." He climbed into the driver's side.

Anna ran to his window. "Esteban, I ..."

"I'm sorry to do this to you, but I don't have time to make other arrangements. You can handle it, can't you?"

Anna smiled weakly. "Oh, sure."

"Good." He kissed her forehead. "I'll get back as quickly as I can."

Dust flew behind the truck as he sped off.

Anna watched until he disappeared from sight, then turned to the children, all of whom were staring at her. "Oh, dear."

Pedro looked at her curiously.

"That was your cousin who just went with the doctor?" she asked.

"Yes."

"Where are your parents?"

"Our mother is dead and our father left."

"What do you mean, he left?"

"He went away one day and didn't come back," the boy said matter-of-factly.

"He just left you children here?"

"Yes."

"And your cousin has been taking care of you?"

"When she's here."

"And who takes care of you when she's not?"

"We take care of ourselves."

Shaking her head, Anna looked around the yard. It was more dirt than grass. Chickens scratched for food. A goat pulled at the already stubby green blades. "How do you normally spend your days?"

Pedro shrugged.

"What about school?"

"We don't go."

"Why not?"

"There isn't one."

Anna was appalled as she looked at each of the children in turn. "Has any of you ever been to school?"

"There was a teacher once, but she left."

Anna shook her head. This was beyond belief—but it wasn't their fault. She looked from one dirty face to another. The cousin might have been looking after them, but she certainly hadn't been taking care of them. "Well, you all look a little the worse for wear. I think the first thing we're going to do is get all of you cleaned up, and then we're going to start doing whatever needs to be done." She looked at Pedro. "Are you the oldest?"

"Yes."

"All right. I'd like you to help me with the younger children. Where do you normally bathe?"

He pointed to a tub of rainwater.

"All right. What about clothes. Do you all have clean clothes?"

"We have other clothes, but they're the same as what we're wearing."

Anna's heart sank. "You mean they're all dirty?"

"Yes."

"Then we must wash them." She hunkered down so that she was eye-level with Pedro. "Can I be honest with you?" she asked softly.

He looked at her suspiciously.

"I've never washed clothing in my life; not even in machines, much less by hand. Can you teach me how?"

Pedro suddenly smiled. "I will show you. It's easy. We'll go to the river."

"Thank you." Anna straightened. "Let's gather up the clothes and anything else that needs to be washed, and we'll all go."

When Anna went into the small house she couldn't believe her eyes. It was messy and dirty. But first things first. She went from bed to bed and ripped off the linen, then started a pile in the middle of the floor that she and the children kept adding to until it was a virtual mountain. Pedro put the clothes into baskets, along with stiff brushes and some homemade soap. Everyone carried what they could, except for Jenetta who grabbed a handful of Anna's skirt and held on as they all trooped single file down a path to a winding river about half a mile away.

The younger children dropped their baskets and jumped into the water. The slightly older ones hung back and waited to be told what to do.

Pedro took his role as head of the family with tremendous seriousness. He made sure that each had his or her own basket and then told them what to do. Anna listened, as well, and started on her own basket, walking into the water, wetting the clothes a piece at a time and scrubbing out the dirt with rocks and brushes. Whenever someone was finished with an item, Pedro would take it and lay it in the sun over bushes or hang it in the trees where the fresh hot breeze could get at it.

When the clothes were finished after what seemed like hours of hard labor, Anna started on the children. One by one, she inspected their necks and ears and rescrubbed the ones that weren't quite clean.

The clothes and linens dried in no time. The kids put on the clean clothes while Anna and Pedro folded everything else and loaded the baskets.

The trip uphill from the river was harder and seemed longer than the trip down had been. Anna set her basket outside the house and had the children do the same.

Then they started the hard work. She lugged the mattresses out of the house and had the children hit them with sticks to get out the dust. They did the same with the handwoven throw rugs that covered the floor.

While they were doing that, Anna started scrubbing. Floors, furniture, walls, everything, until the place began to look and smell clean. Behind the house they started a bonfire to burn all of the trash that had accumulated in and around the house.

Then they brought the mattresses back in and made up the beds with clean linens.

And all the while Anna worked, little Jenetta was never far away, either watching or holding onto the hem of Anna's skirt.

By the time the sun was ready to set, the work was done and everyone was exhausted and hungry. The only thing Anna thought she could make without bungling it was scrambled eggs, which worked out well because eggs were the only fresh food she could find. Pedro collected them and showed her how to start the fire in the old wood-burning stove, and Anna took it from there.

She felt a real sense of pride as the eggs fluffed up in the deep skillet. After spooning them into bowls, she watched the children's faces for their reaction.

To put it mildly, they weren't thrilled, but there was nothing else to eat so they cleaned their bowls.

Anna rinsed everything out, then put the children to bed, four to a mattress. They were exhausted and so was she.

When everyone was down, she quietly stepped outside. There was none of the constant chatter of children that she'd heard all day. None of the constant motion. Everything was peaceful and quiet.

Raising her face to the moonlit sky, she stretched her arms high over her head. There was a sudden tug on her skirt. She looked down to find Jenetta, her thumb, as ever, in her mouth.

Anna smiled softly as she knelt in front of the child. "Couldn't you sleep, sweetheart?" she asked in Spanish.

Jenetta didn't say anything, but she leaned against Anna.

Anna hugged her, then picked her up and carried her into the house. There was a rocking chair next to one of the beds. Anna sat in it with Jenetta and rocked her gently back and forth. She lay in Anna's arms staring up at her. With her free hand, she reached up to touch Anna's silky hair, twirling it around her finger. Ever so slowly, her eyelids began to drift closed.

A soft smile touched Anna's mouth as she watched. Jenetta was so completely lovely.

Still rocking, Anna leaned her head against the back of the chair listening to the steady breathing of the rest of the children.

* * *

It was still dark out when Esteban returned, but hours had passed. When Anna heard his truck stop in front of the house, she watched the door. An older woman with iron-gray hair came in first. She smiled at Anna but didn't say anything. Esteban entered just behind her. He looked around the dimly lit spotless house, then turned to Anna.

"Hello," he said quietly as he crossed the room to her. "You've been busy."

"We all have. How is the girl?"

"She has pneumonia. I left her at the clinic."

"When is she coming back?"

"She isn't. She doesn't want to take care of the children any longer. It's a big responsibility for someone so young."

Anna looked down at Jenetta. "So what happens to them now?"

"I brought back a nurse who's agreed to stay with them until I can make other arrangements."

Already she didn't like the sound of that. "What kind of arrangements?"

"I'm not sure yet. If there's any way to keep the children together, of course I will. But I think they'll probably have to be split up and given to different families."

Anna looked up at him. "You can't do that."

"I'll try not to."

Jenetta, still sleeping, whimpered as though she were having a bad dream. Esteban leaned over Anna's shoulder and smoothed the little girl's hair with a gentle hand, then lifted her from Anna's arms and held her.

He was such a large man; such a stong man—and so completely gentle. Anna felt her throat tighten as she watched him.

As he leaned over the bed to tuck the little girl in between her sisters, Anna rose and walked quickly from the house.

Esteban's eyes followed her curiously as he straightened. After giving the nurse some final instructions, he went outside. Anna was already in the truck, and he climbed in beside her.

"Anna," he said as he sat beside her.

She shook her head. "Please, I don't want to talk."

He looked at her for a long moment. "All right," he said as he started the engine and headed for home.

Anna was silent, staring out the window, watching as the headlights bounced over the landscape, but not really seeing anything. The tightness in her throat worked its way into her chest and stomach and made breathing difficult. She didn't want to be in the truck with Esteban. She didn't want to be anywhere near him. As soon as it stopped in front of his house, she shot out of the passenger door and ran up the steps to her room, slamming the door behind her.

Esteban sat in the truck alone for a time, surprised and yet not surprised at all. He slowly followed Anna upstairs.

She paced from one end of her room to the other. She wanted to scream. She wanted to cry.

Esteban walked in without knocking.

She spun around. "Get out."

"No.

"Please, Esteban." There was a note of pleading in her voice. "I don't want you here right now."

"Then you have a problem, because I'm here and I'm not leaving until we talk."

"Fine." She pulled a suitcase out of the closet, slammed it onto her bed and started tossing clothes into it. "You can watch me pack."

"Why are you so angry?"

"I'm not angry. I just want to get out of here. Desperately."

Esteban grabbed her arm and spun her around to face him. "You don't think I'm going to let you leave here like this, do you?"

"When I choose to leave has nothing to do with you."

"You and I both know that it has everything to do with me."

Anna stopped struggling and looked into his eyes. Hers suddenly filled with tears. "Oh, God."

He cupped her face in his hands. "What is it?"

Anna walked away from Esteban and kept her back toward him until she regained some control. "This wasn't supposed to happen." She turned and her eyes met his. "I wasn't supposed to fall in love with you."

"Yes, you were," he said quietly.

"What?"

"From the moment I met you at the wedding, I intended to make you fall in love with me."

"That doesn't make any sense. You left me there. You never called or wrote or tried to see me."

"I'm a very patient man. I knew you'd come to visit Hayley eventually."

Her eyes looked into his and filled with tears again. "So the time I've spent here has been nothing more than the emotional seduction of Anna Bennett. A game. You must be pleased with your handiwork. I'm sure it succeeded beyond your wildest expectations."

"Anna," he said quietly, "the time you've spent here has been the emotional maturation of Anna Bennett. There's no game involved, believe me. I don't play games."

"You don't play games? Then explain the purpose of all this? What do you mean by emotional maturation?"

"Anna," he said gently, "you're extremely well-traveled, well-educated, very good at your job and the pride of your father's life, and until you came here, you didn't know what it was like to genuinely care about anyone or anything that wasn't connected in some way to you. That's all changed now. You've grown a lot in the short time you've been here."

Anna dashed at her wet cheeks with the back of her hand. "What noble goals. But it would have been kinder of you to leave me the way I was. Nothing has changed except that I used to be happy and now I'm not." She sighed tiredly. "Please, Esteban, go away. Leave me alone."

"Not until I finish what I have to say."

"There's more?"

Esteban stepped in front of her and raised her face to his. "Anna, I told you that this wasn't a game. I fell in love with you the first moment we met. I knew then that I wanted you for my wife, and I knew how difficult that was going to be to achieve.''

Anna's lips parted softly in surprise. ''You love me, too?''

A smile touched his eyes as he pushed her hair behind her ears. ''More than I can begin to tell you. This past year of waiting has been difficult.''

''Why didn't you come to me?''

''Because you weren't ready to love me yet. To be honest, I'm not sure that you're ready now.''

''But I do love you.''

''How much, Anna? How much are you willing to give up for me? And make no mistake. You would have to sacrifice the life you lead now in order to live here and share my life. And as you've learned from firsthand experience, things are difficult here. Much more difficult than anything you're used to.''

''Can't I have my work and love you, too?''

''How? You know as well as I do that your work consumes you. What would you do, visit me on weekends—if you can manage it? That's not a marriage. I want a real home with you. I want to have children with you.''

Anna didn't say anything.

He touched his lips to her forehead. ''If I could, I'd join your world and not force you to make a choice, but I can't. Too many people depend on me here.''

Her heart was in her eyes as she looked up at him. ''How can I possibly make that kind of choice? My father's been training me to take over his corporation since I was a child. I have a responsibility to him. My choosing marriage to you would break his heart."

Esteban trailed his fingers down her cheek. "I can't make this any easier for you. I can only give you whatever time you need to make a decision."

"And if I decide to stay with my father?"

"I'll accept it."

"You wouldn't fight for me even a little?"

"No. Not if it meant hurting you. Your choice isn't really between your father and me. It's between love and responsibility. No matter how much I love you, I could never turn my back on the people here. They are my responsibility, and my being here could mean the difference between life and death for them; between having a home and not having a home. And even knowing all of that, it wasn't an easy choice for me to make because I knew that it might well cost me any kind of future with you."

"I wouldn't want you to try to live in my world. This is where you belong."

"And where do you belong, Anna?"

She shook her head. "If you'd asked me that a week ago, I could have answered without hesitation."

"And now?"

"I don't know any more."

Esteban looked at her suitcase. "When are you leaving?"

"I was planning on calling the airport to send a helicopter for me this morning."

"I see. I'd better let you get on with your packing." He lifted her silky golden hair and let it drift through his fingers. Then he turned to leave.

"Esteban."

He stopped, his back toward her.

"Won't you stay with me until I go?"

He shook his head and turned back to her. "If I do, I might not be able to let you go." His eyes moved tenderly over her face, memorizing each feature. Then without saying anything else, he turned and left.

Anna stood staring at the door as it closed after him. She ached with the need to call him back; to feel his arms close warmly around her.

But she didn't.

Chapter Nine

Anna walked into her father's hotel suite and found him sitting on the couch, dictating to his secretary. He rose as soon as she entered and embraced her. "Hi, honey. Is everything all right? You sounded a little upset when you called."

Anna looked past her father at his secretary. "Hi, Mary. Will you please excuse us for a little while?"

"Of course." She gathered her things and went into another room in the suite, closing the door behind her.

Her father walked to the bar and poured himself a drink. "Do you want anything?"

"No, thanks."

"I hear that Hayley and Marcos are happily settled in with her parents."

"Yes. I talked to her last night."

"And the baby?"

"Due any day."

He sat down on the couch and Anna sat across from him. Her father looked at her curiously. "All right. What's going on?"

She looked down at her clenched hands to collect her thoughts, then looked back at her father. "I've been struggling with something ever since I got back from Spain."

"I know."

"How?"

"You've been very distracted. I assume it has something to do with the good doctor."

"I love him," she said softly.

Her father's expression didn't change, but his mouth hardened into a straight line. "I see."

"He's the most wonderful person I've ever met. I know you'd think so, too, if you'd just get to know him."

"I'll take a rain check."

Anna rose and walked to the window. "I'm going to marry him."

"Oh, for God's sake, Anna, use your head. You can't marry the man. He'd never fit into our world. What would he do?"

She turned back to her father. "He doesn't have to fit into our world, because I'm going to fit into his."

"What?"

"I'm giving you my notice, Dad. I'll stay with the company for as long as it takes to clear up the projects I'm currently working on, but then I'm going to Spain to live."

Her father shook his head as he rose from the couch. "I don't believe what I'm hearing."

Her eyes filled with tears. "I'm sorry. I love you so much, and I know how this must hurt you. These past several weeks have been an agony for me. I hate letting you down. I've spent my entire life trying to live up to what you wanted me to be. But now I have to do what's best for me."

Her father gripped her shoulders in his hands. "Anna, you don't know what you're saying."

"Yes, I do. You and I both know that the company will go on quite successfully without me. But I don't think I can go on at all without Esteban."

"The man is a zero. A nothing. A nobody."

Anna shook her head. "He's everything."

"No. I'm not going to accept this. It's an aberration. You're going to come to your senses, and then everything will be the way it was."

"Dad . . ."

He crossed to the bar and poured himself another drink. "I don't want to talk about it any more tonight. You go on back to your suite. I have some things I need to take care of."

Anna started for the door, but turned back and looked at her father. "Please accept it and try to be happy for me. I'm not going to change my mind."

As soon as the door had closed after her, Charles Bennett opened the door through which his secretary had disappeared. "Mary, get in here."

She came rushing in, wide-eyed at his tone of voice. "Yes?"

"I want you to find the quickest way to get me from here to Esteban Alvarado's home in Spain."

"Yes, sir."

"Now."

"Yes, sir."

"And not a word about this to my daughter. If I'm not back before tomorrow morning, tell her I'm sleeping late, or had an early morning meeting. Whatever sounds convincing."

"Yes, sir. I'll call a maid to pack for you."

"I won't be staying long enough to need a suitcase." He looked at Mary. "What are you standing there for? Get moving."

She rushed from the room hugging her steno pad.

Anna went to her room, unaware of the sudden flurry of activity she'd left behind. She started to call Esteban. Her hand actually hovered over the receiver. But then she withdrew it. She'd purposely not called him since leaving Spain, in an effort to give herself more perspective about things. Right now she was upset, and as much as she wanted to talk to him, she wanted to do it when he wouldn't hear anything but happiness in her voice.

Esteban and two other men were working on a fence near the stables when he heard the helicopter. He watched as it landed in front of the house and sent up a choking cloud of dust that lingered for a few minutes even after the blades had stopped.

He picked up his shirt from a post and wiped the sweat from his face with it as he walked toward the helicopter. Anna's father climbed out and waited for him.

Esteban stopped in front of him. "I assume this visit has something to do with Anna?"

"It has everything to do with her. She came to me a few hours ago to tell me that she's going to marry you."

Esteban didn't say anything.

"And I came here to tell you that she's not."

"It's Anna's decision."

"So it would appear at first glance. Now let me tell you what I'm going to do with Anna if you go through with this. I will disown and disinherit her. She will never again have any contact with her aunt, her uncle, Hayley or myself. Life as she understands it to be will be over. And if you know my daughter, at all, you know that her family is everything to her."

Esteban looked into Charles Bennett's steely eyes. "You would do that to your own daughter?"

"In a minute."

"Does she know?"

"Not yet. I wanted to tell you first."

"Why?"

"Anna is a strange girl at times. If I back her into a corner, she might well sacrifice everything to be with you. But if you, on the other hand, know that she'll be coming to you with only the clothes she's wearing and nothing else, you might be more inclined to break the tie that binds."

"You think I want Anna for her money?"

"That's exactly what I think. You've had your eye on her bank balance since Hayley's wedding. I've been around a long time, Doctor, and I know an opportunist when I meet one." He took a check from his pocket and stuck it in Esteban's hand. "Look at it."

Esteban did. He could have built an entire hospital with that amount.

"You let my daughter go and I'll endorse that check. It'll take care of all your money problems for years to come. You don't let her go and you get nothing."

"So this is the world according to Charles Bennett," Esteban said. "Not a very pretty place." He stuffed the check into the older man's suitcoat pocket, then strode to the helicopter and opened the door. "I want you to leave my property right now."

"I'm not finished."

"Yes, you are."

There was something in Esteban's tone that indicated to the older man he'd better do as he was told.

Without waiting for it to take off, Esteban walked into the house. Carmina came running up to him. "Miss Bennett is on the phone."

"I can't talk to her right now."

"But she's on the phone."

"Tell her I'm not here."

"But . . ."

He leveled his eyes at her. "I said to tell her I'm not here. When you've done that, go home."

"What about your dinner?"

"I don't want any."

She looked at him strangely, but did as he asked.

When the house was empty and silent, he went into the library and sat behind his desk. He stayed there, unmoving, while the sun set, leaving him in total darkness.

The phone rang. He stared at it, knowing without having to answer it, that Anna was at the other end.

And he let it ring and ring until it finally stopped.

Leaning back in his chair, he stared blindly at the ceiling.

Anna spent hours trying to get in touch with Esteban, then finally gave up and went to bed. It was just a little past four in the morning when her phone rang. She groggily reached for it without bothering to turn on her bedside lamp. "Hello?" she said as she lay back on her pillow.

"Hello, Anna."

She opened her eyes and smiled. "Esteban! I've been trying to call you."

"I know."

"I have something to tell you."

"Let me talk first."

Anna rose up on an elbow, a small frown creasing her forehead. "What's wrong?"

"I've been doing a lot of thinking about us, and it isn't going to work."

"What?" she said softly.

"Regardless of what you decide, there isn't going to be a marriage."

"But why?"

There was a long pause. "Like I said, it just isn't going to work."

"But, Esteban, I . . ."

"Look, this has been a difficult call to make. I'm sure it's been just as difficult for you to receive. Let's not drag it out. It's over and there's nothing else to say."

Anna was stunned into silence.

"Goodbye, Anna."

"No! Wait! You don't mean it, Esteban. I know you don't. I'm coming to see you. We can work this out. Any differences we have can be taken care of."

"Don't come here."

"But we have to talk."

"We just did."

"Not like this. Esteban, please, don't do this."

He could hear the anguish in her voice and it tore at his heart. "Anna, let it go. Let me go."

"I can't. And I *am* coming to see you."

Esteban closed his eyes. "I didn't want to say this because I was trying to spare your feelings, but the fact is that I don't love you. I thought I did, but I was wrong. And I don't want you to come here."

"I see," she finally managed to say, stricken.

"I wish all the best for you," he said quietly. "Try to be happy. It's for the best."

The line went dead in her hand. Anna took the receiver away from her ear and stared at it. This wasn't happening. It was all a bad dream.

She hung up and sat on the edge of her bed. She couldn't even cry. It hurt too much.

The phone rang again, almost immediately.

She grabbed the receiver and held it to her ear with both hands. "Esteban?"

"No. It's me, Hayley."

"Hayley?" It took her a moment to focus her thoughts. "Are you all right? Is it the baby?"

"I'm fine. I know it's a horrible hour to call anyone, but I was lying in bed and couldn't sleep, and I just had a feeling that you needed to talk to someone."

Anna shook her head. "I can't talk now."

"What's wrong? Why did you think I was Esteban?"

"He just called. I thought he was calling back."

"Did the two of you fight?"

"Oh, no, there was no fight. He just told me that he's discovered that he doesn't love me, after all."

"Oh, Anna, I'm so sorry."

Her throat tightened so much with emotion that she couldn't speak.

"Did he say what happened to change things?"

Anna cleared her throat. "No."

"That doesn't sound like Esteban."

"Of course it does. He's very honest. To allow me to go on thinking we had a future was a lie. In a strange way, I almost feel sorry for him. He's such a good man. It can't have been easy for him to tell me."

"I'm getting dressed and coming over."

Anna had to smile. "You say that as though Paris were just across the street from New York."

"It almost is, on the Concorde."

"Oh, Hayley, you'd really do that, wouldn't you? Please don't. Aside from the fact that you have no business going anywhere in your condition, I'd rather be alone."

"Are you sure?"

"Yes. As a matter of fact, I don't even want to talk on the phone. It's too much effort."

"All right, but I'm going to call again first thing in the morning."

"It already is first thing in the morning."

"Second thing, then. And if you need me, I'm here for you. Any time."

"I know that, Hayley. Thank you."

She hung up the phone for the second time that morning and walked to her window to look out at the still-dark Paris street. She felt oddly quiet inside. Minutes ago she'd been in more pain than she'd ever felt before, but now she was completely numb. She didn't want to cry; she didn't want to smile. She just wanted to be completely still.

Chapter Ten

Anna was sitting on the lawn with the rest of her family at her aunt and uncle's home, a glass of lemonade in her hand, watching Hayley's four-month-old baby lying asleep on a blanket in front of her.

Charles Bennett sat quietly watching her. She'd changed a lot in the past several months. It wasn't anything overt. She still looked the same. Her work was still good and very thorough. But now when she smiled, it never quite seemed to reach her eyes. He couldn't remember the last time he'd heard her laugh out loud.

Things would get better, of course. He was convinced he'd done the right thing. Anna and that Alvarado man? He couldn't imagine a worse match for her. But watching her the way she was now tugged at his heart.

Hayley picked up her baby and cuddled him. "Can you believe this?" she asked with a beaming smile. "Can you believe I'm really a mother?"

"It does seem strange. I can't even imagine what it must be like to suddenly find yourself so completely responsible for another human being." She looked at her cousin's profile. "Do you ever miss it?"

"Miss what?"

"Spain. The ranch."

Hayley adjusted the baby's blanket and looked at her husband. "A little, at times."

"A lot," Marcos said, speaking for himself. "It's my home. It always will be."

"That's absurd. What's to miss?" Anna's father asked. "From what I could see, it's little more than dirt and hard, sweaty work. And after all that work you come back to some little cracker box of a house. Even the flowers in the window planters are wilted and dying, and that's exactly what would happen to anyone crazy enough to stay there."

Anna looked at her father, suddenly alert.

"Frankly, the biggest sin, as far as I'm concerned," he continued, "is that there's no return for all that hard work. It's a complete waste of time and effort."

Anna looked at her father curiously. "How do you know what the house looks like?"

"What?"

"How do you know what the house looks like?"

He waved his hand as though it had no importance. "You must have told me."

"I've never discussed it with you."

"Then Hayley or Marcos must have said something."

"About wilted flowers in the window planters?" She looked at Marcos and Hayley. They both shrugged. Anna turned back to her father. "When were you there?"

"Anna, I . . ."

"When were you there?" she demanded.

Charles Bennett sighed as he looked at his daughter. "You're not going to drop this, are you?"

"When were you there?"

"About four months ago."

"Why?"

"I had some business to discuss with the good doctor."

"Business? Was I, by any chance, that business?"

"Anna, I don't want to talk about this. Any discussion that took place was between Dr. Alvarado and myself, and I'd like it to remain that way."

"Did you and Esteban talk about me?"

"Yes."

"When was this?"

"I told you. About four months ago."

"Precisely when?" Anna was a good and determined interrogator. Her father had taught her well.

"The day after you told me you intended to marry him."

Her voice was cold and flat—stripped of all emotion. "What did you say to him?"

"I gave him a check and told him to leave you alone."

That wasn't the answer she was expecting, and it hit her like a blow. "You gave him money in exchange for me?"

Marcos rose from his chair. "You're lying. My brother would never take money from you."

The older man ignored the younger one. His attention was focused entirely on his daughter. "Anna, honey, I did what was best for you. You weren't thinking clearly at the time, so I had to do your thinking for you."

"Did he take the money?"

Her father's eyes shifted, but just for a moment. "No," he finally said quietly, "he didn't."

Anna closed her eyes. She'd already known what the answer was going to be, but hearing her father say it aloud made it real. Opening her eyes, she focused on her father. "Then why did he call me? Why did he break off our relationship?"

"You want the whole story, don't you? All right, here it is. He broke off your relationship because I told him that if he married you, I'd disown and disinherit you and make sure you never saw any of your family again."

Anna's pain-filled eyes looked into those of her father's. "You told him that?"

"Yes."

"Is it true? Would you really do that to me for just marrying the man I love?"

Charles Bennett didn't speak for a moment. His mouth grew tight. "For marrying Esteban Alvarado, yes, I would. And you've worked with me long enough to know that I don't make idle threats, Anna."

Hayley rose indignantly to her feet. "You can't order me not to see Anna."

He swung his attention to his niece. "Your father heads up one of my companies, young lady. I can take it away from him just as easily as I gave it to him. The same, I might add, goes for your husband and that nice little job your father gave him."

Anna's Aunt Catherine looked at her husband and gently touched his hand. Then she looked at her brother, searing him with her intensity. "Charles, your behavior is despicable."

"My behavior may be despicable, as you say, but you'll back me up, Catherine, because you have no choice."

Catherine stormed into the house. Her husband, ever calm, leaned forward, his elbows on his knees. "Charles, you're not being reasonable. If you heard someone who was working for you talking the way you're talking now, you'd fire him."

"I won't have Anna marrying that man. I'll do whatever it takes to keep it from happening." He turned to his daughter, angrier than he could ever remember being before. "That man is nothing but trouble. I knew it the first time I met him. I will not allow you to be with him."

Anna rose, her eyes on her father, so filled with hurt and disappointment that she could barely speak.

"Where are you going?"

"To Spain, where I should have been all along," she said quietly.

"I meant what I said. I'll disinherit you. You won't get a penny."

"You can keep your pennies, Dad. I know how much they mean to you."

"Anna..."

She shook her head. "I can't believe you would betray me like this, but I suppose I shouldn't really be surprised. Money has always meant everything to you. My mistake was in believing that I meant something to you apart from the money."

"Anna, you're my daughter and I love you."

"No, Dad. You own me. At least you used to. I don't need your money any more. I don't even want it." She looked at the sky for a moment and then back at her father. "I'm amazed at my misguided sense of responsibility. I was so worried about hurting you or disappointing you that I almost gave up Esteban on my own."

"He's nothing, Anna."

"He's *everything*," she said softly. "If you'd ever bothered to get to know him you would have found him to be a man of honor and integrity who makes more of a contribution to the world than you or I could ever hope to." Her gaze moved over her father's face. "Goodbye, Dad."

"Anna," he yelled after her retreating back. "I meant what I said. You'll get nothing. If you go to him, you'll go with nothing."

It was still light out when the helicopter landed in front of the hacienda. Anna climbed out with her single suitcase and waved it away, then ran inside and into Carmina. The housekeeper's face lit up at the sight of her. "You're back!"

"To stay this time. Where's Esteban?"

"He had to go to the village. He won't be back until late tonight."

"Oh." She sounded as disappointed as she felt.

"He'll be so happy to see you. He's been different since you left."

"Different how?"

Carmina shrugged. "Just different. How long are you staying?"

"For as long as he'll let me."

The housekeeper smiled. "I'll get your room ready," she said as she took Anna's suitcase and went upstairs.

Anna went outside and walked around, down to the stables and out to the ruins. For the first time in her life, she felt like she was truly home.

When she got back to the house she had a small dinner, then curled up on the couch in the library with a book to wait.

And wait she did. It was after midnight when she heard the truck stop outside. Anticipation bubbled up inside her when she heard his footsteps in the hall. And then he was there. He came into the library to turn out the light and saw Anna sitting on the couch, her legs curled beneath her, a book on her lap. For a long time he just looked at her, his eyes moving over every feature of her face. "What are you doing here?" he finally asked.

"I came to be with you, if you'll let me."

"Anna, I told you on the phone..."

She put the book on the couch next to her and rose. "I know what you told me, and now I know why." She crossed the room to stand in front of him. "You love me as much as you ever did."

He didn't say anything.

She moved closer. "I'm not leaving you. Not ever again."

"You don't know what you're saying."

She raised up on her toes and kissed him.

Esteban stood still and straight.

She circled her arms around his neck as she looked into his eyes. "How could you not know how much I love you?" she whispered against his mouth.

"You shouldn't be here."

"I should be wherever you are."

He raised his hands to her face and looked into her eyes. "Are you sure you know what you're doing?"

"I've never been more sure of anything in my life."

"Oh, Anna," he said softly as he wrapped her in his arms and held her. "I've missed you so much."

"I'm never leaving you again."

"What about your father?"

She raised her head and looked at him. "I don't want anything more to do with him. Not until he can accept the two of us together."

"That may never happen."

"I know."

"He'll be lost to you."

"That's his choice."

"And the money? Are you going to be able to live like this after the way you've been brought up?"

"Don't you see that that's not important?"

"What I see is that the life you're about to step into is a lot harder than the life you're leaving behind."

She shook her head. "Nothing could be harder than living without you. You make me feel things. You give me life. You made me realize how empty my world really was before you came into it."

Esteban touched the corner of her mouth with his thumb. "I thought my life was full. I had my work, my ranch, a sense of purpose. And then you crashed into me in the hallway at your aunt's house, and in that moment my world as I knew it to be disappeared. It was as though I'd been searching for you without realizing it, and then suddenly you were there. Just being with you brought me such joy. And I wanted you to love me, too."

"I did. I just didn't recognize it for what it was."

"I never meant to cause you pain."

"The only pain came when you said you didn't love me."

"The words were like a knife through my own heart, but it was the only way I knew to keep you away. If you'd come here, I could never have looked into your eyes and said the words." He kissed her forehead. "I'm so sorry about your family."

"Don't be. It's not your fault."

His eyes moved over her lovely face. "Well, Anna Bennett, how would you feel about marrying a poor country doctor with absolutely no prospects to speak of?"

"I've never wanted anything more in my life."

He shook his head. "How is it possible to love so much? You've become the reason I breathe; the reason my heart beats. It's frightening, this power you have over me." He raised her face to his with a gentle finger under her chin.

Anna ached with happiness. She and Esteban were meant to be together. A fate like that couldn't be denied. And Esteban was her fate. Her destiny. Nothing else mattered.

Epilogue

Anna gazed into the crib at her sleeping son. Reaching out a gentle hand, she touched his dark hair. He was the image of his father except for his eyes. Those had come from her.

Esteban, dressed only in his drawstring pajama bottoms, leaned his shoulder against the doorframe and watched. After three years, he still thought Anna was the most exquisite woman he'd ever seen. His love for her had grown deeper and richer until he no longer knew where he stopped and she began. There wasn't anything he wouldn't do for her.

Anna sensed her husband's presence. Turning her head, her eyes met his and filled with such love that it took his breath away. He crossed the room and took her into his arms. "Good morning," he said softly as he nuzzled her ear.

"Morning."

"How's Adan?"

"Still sleeping," she whispered.

"You should be, too. The sun isn't even up yet."

"I'm not tired."

He cupped her face in his hands. "Is everything all right, Anna?"

Her eyes met his. "I love you."

He rubbed his thumb over her lips. "I know."

"And though I wouldn't change anything I've done, I sometimes miss my father. I'd like to be able to share our happiness with him." She turned in Esteban's arms and leaned the back of her head against his bare chest as she gazed at their month old son. "I think he must be very lonely."

"He's done it to himself, Anna. He could have come here with your aunt and uncle, and Hayley and Marcos when our child was born, but he chose not to."

"I know," she said softly. "He's so proud. I don't think he knows how to back down."

Esteban rubbed his morning-rough cheek against her silky hair. "Maybe one of these days he'll figure it out." He turned Anna to face him in the circle of his arms. "In the meantime, I forgot to tell you that I'm going on a trip. I'll be gone for two or three days."

"Where to?"

"Just to the big city. I want to check out some medical equipment for the clinic."

"You told me about that. Isn't some doctor retiring or something like that?"

"Um-hmm. And he's selling everything. It's not state of the art, but it's better than nothing, and the price is right."

"Are you going to bring it back with you?"

"No. I don't want it bouncing around the back of the pick up truck. I'll have to have it flown in."

"That's expensive."

"We'll eat lots of rice for the next year," he said with a smile.

"I don't mind."

His gaze roamed over her lovely face. "That's the wonder. You never do."

Anna's eyes sparkled. "You're a lucky man to have found such a gem for a wife."

He smiled also, then grew serious as he lowered his lips to hers in a long, lingering kiss. Leaning his forehead against hers, he sighed. "I have to shower and dress."

Anna kissed the corner of his mouth and worked her way to his ear. "You can stay a little longer," she said softly.

"Oh, Anna," he groaned, "don't do that. It's too soon after Adan."

"I feel fine."

"I'm the doctor," he said as he moved away from her, his hands on her shoulders, "and I want you to have a few more weeks to recover. It was a difficult birth."

"All right. I'll be good."

Esteban went to the crib and stood looking down at his son. After a moment, he leaned over and placed a kiss on the baby's chubby pink cheek. "You take good care of your mama, Adan. I'll be back soon.'' Straightening, he looked at his wife. "And you, my love, should go back to sleep.''

"I will. I just want to stay here for a little longer.''

Esteban kissed her once more, then quietly left the room and went to his library. After closing the door behind him, he picked up the phone and dialed. Minutes passed before his brother answered at the other end. "Marcos, I need to know where Anna's father is . . .''

Charles Bennett stared out the window of his Rome hotel suite. There was a knock on the door. He heard his secretary's voice and then silence. "Mary,'' he said without turning around, "who was it?''

"Me.''

He turned abruptly to find Esteban standing ten feet away. "What are you doing here?''

"We need to talk.''

The older man crossed the room to his desk and sat down. "I have nothing to say to you.''

"Then you can listen. Four weeks ago, Anna gave birth to your grandson. We named him Adan Charles.''

He sat in silence for a long time. "I didn't know,'' he finally said quietly.

"Anna wrote telling you, but you returned her letter unopened.'' Esteban took a picture of Anna holding Adan and put it on the desk.

The other man didn't touch it, but his gaze was riveted. "Why, exactly, are you here, Alvarado?''

"Because Anna is worried about you. She wants you to be a part of our lives. She wants you to know your grandson and for your grandson to know you."

"Did she send you?"

"No. Anna has no idea that I've come here. I didn't want her to be disappointed if I failed."

"I see."

"I neither want nor do I expect a response from you now. I just want you to know that Anna and I will welcome you to our home if you should choose to come." With that, Esteban inclined his head and turned to leave.

"Alvarado?"

He turned back.

"Why did you come here after all that's passed between us?"

"Because I love Anna," he said quietly, "and Anna loves you."

When the younger man had gone, Charles Bennett picked up the photograph and leaned back in his chair. His eyes moved over the pretty face of his daughter. Her eyes shone with happiness. And the baby—his grandson. He moved his finger over the baby's face. He was a handsome little guy.

Mary poked her head out of the adjoining room. "May I come in?"

He waved her into the seat across from him. "Mary," he said sternly, "if you ever again let anyone into my presence without my express permission, I'll fire you."

"Yes, sir."

He handed her the picture. "Look at my grandson."

Mary set her notepad on her lap and looked at the photograph. "Oh, Mr. Bennett, he's handsome. He looks just like his father."

"Nonsense," he said gruffly as he snatched the picture from her. "Except for the hair, he's the image of me when I was a baby."

A smile tugged at her mouth. "Yes, sir."

He looked at her suspiciously, then back at the picture. "I really blew it this time."

"There's nothing you've done that can't be changed."

"I can't show up in Spain, hat in hand. It's too much like an admission that I was wrong."

"But you *were* wrong. Your son-in-law has offered you a graceful way out and I think you should take it."

Charles Bennett's eyes narrowed on the woman across from him. "Were you listening at the door?"

"Yes, sir."

"Good. I don't have to repeat what was said."

"What are you going to do?"

He sighed. "I don't know, Mary. I just don't know."

Anna, the baby in her arms, stood outside talking to Esteban. She looked up at the noise of a helicopter approaching and shaded her eyes from the sun with a raised hand. "Do you suppose that's some of the medical equipment?" she asked.

Esteban shook his head as he placed his arm around her shoulders. "It's not due here until next week, and it's coming by plane, not helicopter."

They continued watching as it landed away from the house, churning up dust. A man alighted and ducked his head as he walked away from the rotating blades. Anna's lips parted softly. "It's Dad."

The helicopter took off as her father made his steady way toward them. He stopped several yards away and looked at his daughter. "Hello, Anna," he said softly.

She swallowed hard. "What are you doing here?"

"I thought it was time to let go of the past. I've missed you."

"I've missed you, too."

"I'm sorry about everything. My behaviour has been inexcusable."

A tremulous smile touched her mouth. "You're here now. That's all that matters."

He looked at the baby in her arms. "I'd like to meet my grandson, if that's all right."

"Of course."

He set down his suitcase and walked toward her. Anna carefully handed Adan to him. The baby didn't seem to mind at all. When her father touched his grandson's hand, the baby's tiny fingers curled around his pinky. The older man's eyes filled with tears as he looked at his daughter. "He's beautiful, Anna." Then he looked at Esteban. "Thank you."

Esteban inclined his dark head and pulled Anna closer to his side.

Anna looked up at her husband. "You did this, didn't you?" she asked quietly.

"Your father did it. All I did was invite him."

Her eyes met and held his. "You are the most wonderful man and I'm the luckiest woman in the world."

Esteban kissed her forehead. "All I want is for you to be happy."

She leaned her head against his shoulder as she watched her father cooing at the baby. "This is like the icing on the cake."

Charles Bennett looked up from his grandson. "He's smiling. But it's not a silly smile. It's a very intelligent smile. I can tell already that he has the makings of a fine businessman."

"Dad..."

He grinned. "Just kidding—kind of."

Anna walked over to her father. "Adan is going to be whatever he wants to be."

Her father nodded. "And that's the way it should be." He kissed his daughter on the cheek. "I'm sorry it took me so long to figure that out."

"It doesn't matter how long it took. It only matters that you did."

Charles looked at her for a long moment, then nodded. "I won't make the same mistake a second time. And as for this little guy," he said, looking back at his grandson, "I think it's too hot out here. I'm going to take him inside."

Anna started to follow them into the house, but Esteban caught her hand and swung her around into his arms. "Kiss me."

She wound her arms around his neck. "With pleasure."

Esteban's lips came down on hers in a long, slow kiss. "Ummm," he said after a moment. "That was nice."

"It gets nicer."

He smiled and kissed the tip of her nose. "Oh, I know."

Anna gazed into her husband's eyes.

"What?" he asked quietly.

"I didn't know it was possible to be this happy."

"I knew it the moment I saw you, and I haven't doubted it a moment since."

With their arms around each other, they walked into their home.

* * * * *

COMING NEXT MONTH

#730 BORROWED BABY—Marie Ferrarella
A Diamond Jubilee Book!
Stuck with a six-month-old bundle of joy, reserved policeman Griff Foster became a petrified parent. Then bubbly Liz MacDougall taught him a thing or two about diapers, teething, lullabies and love.

#731 FULL BLOOM—Karen Leabo
When free-spirited Hilary McShane returned early from her vacation, she hadn't expected to find methodical Matthew Burke as a substitute house-sitter. Their life-styles and attitudes clashed, but their love kept growing....

#732 THAT MAN NEXT DOOR—Judith Bowen
New dairy owner Caitlin Forrest was entranced by friendly neighbor Ben Wade. When she discovered that he wanted her farm, however, she wondered exactly how much business he was mixing with pleasure.

#733 HOME FIRES BURNING BRIGHT—Laurie Paige
Book II of HOMEWARD BOUND DUO
Carson McCumber felt he had nothing to offer a woman—especially privileged Tess Garrick. Out to prove the rugged rancher wrong, Tess was determined to keep all the home fires burning....

#734 BETTER TO HAVE LOVED—Linda Varner
Convinced she'd lose, loner Allison Kendall had vowed never to play the game of love. But martial-arts enthusiast Meade Duran was an expert at tearing down all kinds of defenses.

#735 VENUS de MOLLY—Peggy Webb
Cool, controlled banker Samuel Adams became hot under the collar when he thought about his mother marrying Molly Rakestraw's father. But that was before he met the irrepressible Molly!

AVAILABLE THIS MONTH: